1

I love Mondays! thought seventeen-year-old Jane Ryan as she sat at the kitchen table casually sipping her green tea and reading the morning edition of the *Welling Pointe Post* – her usual before-school routine.

She took in the headline on page three – "Vandals Trigger Heightened Neighbourhood Watch" – and read the story. It seemed affluent homeowners in the gated community of Stone Water Bend on Long Island, New York, were fed up with the slow police response to a recent rash of vandalism. Now the residents were organised and taking the matter into their own hands.

"Vandalism?" she murmured. "Why would anyone do something so stupid and destructive? What a waste of time." Then Jane's alarm watch beeped. *Time for school.* She closed the community paper and folded it into a nice, neat square.

"Where *is* it?" Roxy cried, storming through the kitchen for the second time that morning. She flung open the junk drawer and proceeded to tear through it. "I'll *die* if I don't find it!"

Jane had to shake her head. Sometimes the fact that she and Roxy were twins boggled her mind. Exhibit A: Jane was fully dressed in a smart, neutral-coloured outfit by a designer who knew better than to think that every girl wanted to walk out of the house looking like a pop star. Plus, Jane had already exercised, eaten a healthful breakfast, brushed her teeth, and written in her day planner a list of things to do – in order of importance, of course.

Meanwhile Roxy was stalking the house in her oversize Beatles T-shirt that doubled as a nightgown, looking as if she had just rolled out of bed, which she had.

"Where's what?" Jane asked, grabbing the latest issue of the *South Side High Times*, her school newspaper, from the table. Maybe she'd have time to read it on the bus.

"My iPod!" Roxy shrieked. "I can't find it anywhere!"

"When did you last see it?" Jane asked, glancing at the front page of the paper. The smiling image of Derek Shafer stopped her cold. Whoa. It was hard to believe that a guy this hot was athletic and funny *and* smart. But he was. And his picture looked as if he was smiling right at her.

Dream on, Jane thought. Derek had to be every

.E

minute

the secret of jane's success

the secret of jane's success

by Kylie Adams

Based on the characters
created by Emily Fox
from the motion picture *New York Minute*

📚HarperEntertainment
An Imprint of HarperCollins*Publishers*

A PARACHUTE PRESS BOOK

PARACHUTE PRESS

Parachute Publishing, L.L.C.
156 Fifth Avenue
New York, NY 10010

DUALSTAR PUBLICATIONS

Dualstar Publications
1801 Century Park East
12th Floor
Los Angeles, CA 90067

First published in the USA by HarperEntertainment 2004
First published in Great Britain by HarperCollinsEntertainment 2004
HarperCollins*Entertainment* is an imprint of HarperCollins*Publishers* Ltd,
77 – 85 Fulham Palace Road, Hammersmith, London W6 8JB

Book created and produced by Parachute Publishing, L.L.C., in cooperation with
Dualstar Publications, a division of Dualstar Entertainment Group, Inc.

The HarperCollins children's website address is
www.harpercollinschildrensbooks.co.uk

The Mary-Kate and Ashley website address is
www.mary-kateandashley.com

1 3 5 7 9 10 8 6 4 2

ISBN 0 00 718317 8

Printed and bound in Great Britain by Clays Ltd, St Ives plc high school girl's fantasy come to life. And here he was motoring into the school parking lot in his brand-new SUV. This act had earned him "Cool Move of the Week" honours, a distinction announced on the South Side High's school website and in its newspaper.

"You'll probably want to close your mouth," Roxy said, "otherwise you might drool all over that picture."

Jane glanced up, embarrassed, feeling her cheeks turn pink. "What are you talking about? I'm reading the article."

Roxy grinned. "Uh, there is no article. Just a one-line caption." She began riffling through the other newspaper, almost turning over Jane's FUTURE CEOS OF AMERICA mug.

"Roxy!" Jane cried as tea sloshed onto the table. "Watch it!"

"What's your problem?" Roxy asked. She looked down at the picture of Derek, then back at Jane. "Oh, never mind. I get it."

"Get what?" Jane demanded.

Then, as if Roxy suddenly had all the time in the world, she plopped down into the chair next to Jane. "Look. Don't worry about it. I figured it out. You're depressed. You think it's hopeless. You think you'll never have a chance— "

"*What* are you talking about?" Jane cut in.

Roxy tapped on Derek's model-perfect face. "I'm talking about *him*."

Jane did *not* want to have this conversation.

But Roxy pressed on. "You always say that school gossip is a waste of time, but it actually can be very informative. Derek and Faith broke up. They're history. She's even got a new boyfriend. Some college guy. Her parents are freaking out."

Okay, maybe Jane *did* want to have this conversation. "Since when?"

"Since late last night," Roxy said. "I got a zillion instant messages about it. You were already asleep."

Jane tried to play it cool. "That's too bad. They were a cute couple." But the truth was, Jane couldn't wait to talk to her friends on the cheerleading squad about this. Those girls would definitely have the scoop.

"*Cute couple?*" Roxy echoed, rolling her eyes. "They were completely vomitocious. Either all over each other or in a huge fight."

Jane grinned at her sister. "Is *vomitocious* even a word?"

"Well, if it's not, it should be," Roxy replied with a shrug.

Jane glanced at the clock, then back at Roxy. "Do you ever plan on getting dressed? You're going to be late for school."

Roxy rolled her eyes. "Who cares about being on time? I'm already stuck with office assistant hours for the next few weeks. I have to work off demerits during my free periods. What's one more day at Mrs. McCall's photocopy machine?"

Jane said nothing as she folded up the school newspaper and placed it in her backpack. Ever since their mother died two years ago, Roxy seemed to be less and less interested in school. Their dad was an obstetrician and was always busy delivering babies, and Jane could do only so much to encourage her sister. After all, pushing Roxy in a particular direction usually sent her racing in the opposite one.

A thought flashed into Jane's mind. "Try the freezer," she told Roxy.

"Huh?"

"For your iPod," Jane said. "You left it in there once before. Remember?"

Roxy perked up. "And I *did* eat half a pint of Cookie Dough Explosion last night!" She dashed to the freezer. "Yes!" she screamed, waving the cold iPod like a victory flag. "Now I can listen to Rules of Modesty on the way to prison. Did I say *prison*? I meant *school*." She laughed a little.

Jane stood up and smoothed her skirt.

"Why so dressed up?" Roxy asked. Then she gasped. "Oh, my God! Is it Career Day already? I totally forgot. And I was supposed to write the essay for Mr. Vaughn. Oops. Maybe I should stay home today. Tell everybody I have the flu."

"Relax," Jane said, starting to gather her things. "Career Day is next month. Anyway, today is much bigger than that." She beamed proudly. "Today I start as an intern on Congresswoman Kate Kelso's re-election campaign."

"Are you serious?" Roxy asked. Then her eyes took on a glazed look. "Because that sounds really, really boring."

Jane laughed off the teasing. "Well, what may be *boring* to you is *opportunity* for me. I've got the summer college program in D.C. under my belt, and now I'm going to intern for the congresswoman." She cleared her throat. "All important steps if I want to win the McGill Fellowship."

"Please!" Roxy begged. "At least let me be fully awake before you start in on that again."

"But—"

"I know," Roxy cut in. "The McGill Fellowship – a superhard-to-get scholarship to Oxford University. I get it."

"Do you also 'get' how competitive the applicant field is? Students from all over the country are applying," Jane said. "That's why every extracurricular activity is so important. This position on the congresswoman's campaign could be a real boost for my application. She took on only three high school interns, and Millie McDonnell and I got two of those slots."

Roxy started to laugh.

Jane looked at her. "What's so funny?"

"I'm just worried about the rest of the people in the campaign office, that's all," Roxy said. "Between you and Millie, nobody stands a chance. And that includes the congresswoman."

"What is *that* supposed to mean?" Jane asked.

"Well, you're you," Roxy began. "Miss Captain-of-Everything at South Side High – cheerleading squad, debate team – need I go on? And Millie… well, some people think this class-president race is going to her head a little bit."

Jane waved off the notion. "Oh, please. Millie is Millie. She hasn't changed a bit."

"Glad to hear it," Roxy said. "Because there's no reason she should. Everybody knows that Derek Shafer is going to win that election. Every girl who thinks he's a hottie will vote for him. And every guy who wants to be his friend will vote for him too. That leaves Millie with one vote. Assuming she votes for herself, of course." Roxy smiled.

Jane shook her head. "You are in rare form this morning."

"Well, who are you voting for?" Roxy teased. "Your good friend or your secret love?"

"Do you even have to ask?" Jane countered,

pretending not to be bothered as she made her way out of the door. But the truth was that Roxy had hit a nerve. Granted, Millicent McDonnell was a close friend, but Jane had had a mad crush on Derek Shafer since freshman year. He was beyond cute, and he really would be a great class president...

Ugh! Jane stopped that train of thought dead in its tracks. Then she scolded herself. *Bad friend. Very bad friend.* She owed her loyalty to Millie. No matter how much of a hottie Derek was.

2

"Well, this is it," Millie told Jane as they arrived at Congresswoman Kelso's re-election headquarters. "Our first real political campaign. Can you believe it?"

Jane nodded. "This is such a great opportunity," she said, still sitting in Millie's car. "And imagine how amazing a letter of recommendation from the congresswoman would be!"

"I know. Do you remember Ella Biskind?" Millie asked.

The name sounded familiar. "She was a senior last year, right?" Jane asked.

Millie nodded. "I heard Congresswoman Kelso's letter got her into Yale."

"No!" Jane exclaimed.

"Yes!" Millie said. "In fact, I heard that she actually got rejected but that her application was *reconsidered* after the letter came in."

"That is major pull," Jane said. Right away her mind began to race. Could such a letter improve *her* chances of winning the McGill Fellowship to Oxford?

"Oh, I almost forgot," Millie said, pulling something out of her backpack and handing it to Jane. "Just in case you need a sugar rush."

Jane stared at the individually wrapped home-baked cookie in her palm. Attached was a bright pink label that read: VOTE MILLIE FOR THE "SWEET" SIDE LEADERSHIP. She smiled at her friend who had wildly curly auburn hair and freckles. "Very slick, Millie. You're reaching out to every voter's sweet tooth. I'm impressed."

"Thanks," Millie said. Then she sighed heavily. "Now remind me again why I decided to run against the most popular guy in the universe? Was it for the humiliation?"

Jane laughed. "I believe it was for the résumé building." She opened the passenger door of the car. "Shall we?"

Millie nodded. "Don't want to be late on our first day."

Just as they approached the front door, it burst open. A guy who looked to be in his twenties struggled with a huge box of doorknob hangers. He set it down just outside the door. He nodded to Jane and Millie. "Let me guess. High school interns."

"Is it that obvious?" Jane asked, slightly disappointed that she didn't appear to be older and more professional.

"The Sunday-best wardrobe gave you away. Once you get a taste of the real grunt work of a campaign, you'll show up in jeans." He grinned. "I'm Tim Goldsmith, Congresswoman Kelso's press secretary." He gestured to the box he'd just put down. "Interns always get door-to-door hanging duty. Come on," Tim said, waving them inside. "I'll show you guys around."

He led them into the headquarters, where there was a steady rumble of intense activity. Phones were ringing, fax machines were churning out pages, and people were buzzing around in RE-ELECT KATE KELSO T-shirts.

Jane's heart beat like a drum. This was like having a backstage pass at a rock concert. She tried to take in everything yet rein in her excitement at the same time. After all, she had a job to do, and she had to do it well.

"So you're the girls from South Side, right?" Tim asked.

"Yes, sir," Jane said.

"Call me Tim," he said, cutting her off. "You're Melinda and Jane, right?" he added, consulting a bulky gadget and tapping the screen with a tiny stylus.

Millie took a step forward. "Actually, it's Millicent – *Millie*."

Jane peered down to get a better look at Tim's electronic device. It was about twice the size of a

Palm Pilot – larger keypad, larger colour screen. Suddenly it started to ring.

Tim raised a hand in a halting gesture and pressed a button on his headset mike. "Tim Goldsmith here... Hi, Rita... The congresswoman can do the interview at five-fifteen... Sorry, can't move it. She's got a thirty-minute media window, and Channel Five is already confirmed for the top of the hour... Okay, we'll see you there."

Tim regarded Jane and Millie once more. "We've got time for a quick introduction to the congresswoman, okay?"

The girls nodded eagerly.

"After that it's envelope-stuffing duty. There are ten thousand pieces of mail to get out by the end of the day." He took off.

Jane and Millie rushed to catch up, following him straight into the inner sanctum of Congresswoman Kate Kelso.

The first female congressional seat winner for the fourth district in Long Island history sat behind a massive desk, engaged in a heated phone conversation. "You tell the senator that she's got a fight on her hands. I'm not backing down. I promised the school district those funds, and I intend to deliver." She returned the receiver to the cradle with a bang and looked up.

Jane stood there in awe. This woman represented

real power. Most politicians caved in on issues when they were facing a re-election battle. But Kelso obviously knew how to face down the major players, no matter what was at stake.

Tim made the introductions.

The congresswoman beamed. "Glad you're on board, girls. This place could use some youthful energy." She gave Jane a quick once-over. "Nice suit."

Jane beamed proudly. "Thank you."

Kelso reached for her paper Java Hut cup, realised it was empty, and tossed it into the wastebasket. "I need my afternoon double latte. Who wants to make a coffee run?"

"I do!" Millie blurted out.

The congresswoman smiled. "Eagerness. That's a good sign."

Millie grinned and took off.

Jane was happy for Millie but secretly wished she had spoken up first. Now the congresswoman might think she was lazy! There had to be a way to turn this around. She thought fast, sizing up the scene. Kelso's desk appeared to be in total disarray. "Maybe I could help out here." She gestured to the desk. "I'm a whiz at organising."

The congresswoman shared a smile with Tim. "You wouldn't be the first person who's tried. I'm afraid you're dealing with a hopeless case."

Jane felt a boost of adrenaline. This desk was no way near as cluttered as her father's had once been, and she had whipped that into shape in a few hours.

"*This*," she said confidently, "is not a problem."

While Tim and Kelso discussed a media statement in Tim's office, Jane worked on the congresswoman's desk at a brisk pace, filing, sorting, and transferring stuff to empty file boxes she'd discovered in a corner.

By the time Tim stepped back in, she was almost finished.

"Wow!" Tim exclaimed. "I've never seen her desk this clean."

Jane smiled.

"Your friend's back from Java Hut. I've already got her started on a mailing. Why don't you go give her a hand?"

"Sure," Jane chirped, mindful to keep an upbeat tone in her voice. She wanted to accept every assignment with eagerness. After all, enthusiasm would go a long way towards a great recommendation.

Congresswoman Kelso rushed back into her office, looking flushed. "Tim, Senator Garner just bailed as the luncheon keynote for the League of Women Voters meeting tomorrow. They want me to pinch-hit. Make it work."

A look of panic hit Tim's face. "Impossible. You're overbooked as it is. There's no way."

Jane rocketed into action, flipping open the congresswoman's bulging day planner on her desk to check out the situation, comparing it with an updated printed schedule she had found.

Pangs of nervous energy ticked up Jane's heartbeat. But this was her chance to shine.

Be respectfully assertive, she thought. It's the only way to get noticed.

"Actually, I think it could work," Jane said.

Kelso and Tim looked at her.

Jane swallowed hard, then jumped into the deep end, praying her idea wouldn't get her tossed out of the door. "I'm on the mailing list for the league. That event is being held at the Twain Gallery, right?" She conjured up the nerve to go on.

Tim nodded, narrowing his gaze.

"Well, the Chamber of Commerce luncheon starts half an hour earlier. The congresswoman is just doing the introduction for the new president, and the Durkin Hotel is only five minutes from the Twain Gallery. She could slip out of the Chamber of Commerce once the meal is served and deliver the keynote speech for the league with several minutes to spare."

Tim looked annoyed, ignored Jane, and addressed the congresswoman. "You also have a speech during that hour at the UPS Service Centre. That's a big labour pool. We need their votes."

Jane took a deep breath and spoke up again. "Exactly. That's why I would reschedule the UPS speech for the morning, before their first shift starts. Show up with coffee and doughnuts. They'll appreciate the gesture and listen to what the congresswoman has to say. Arriving at lunchtime would cut into their break. After half a day's hard work, they might resent the intrusion and pay less attention."

Congresswoman Kelso grinned broadly at Jane, then raised her eyebrows at Tim. "I think we have some rescheduling to do."

Tim grinned at Jane, his eyes lit with amusement. "Are you trying to steal my job?" he asked, but he darted out before she could answer.

Then the congresswoman's gaze turned to her desk. "This is amazing. Did someone show up with a dump truck?"

Jane laughed. "It wasn't that bad. Just needed a little organisation."

"You're quick," Kate Kelso said. "I like that. It's refreshing."

"Thanks," Jane said.

"A girl like you must have some pretty ambitious goals. What are your college plans?" the congresswoman asked.

"Oxford University," Jane said, "for the economics programme – assuming I get the McGill Fellowship, that is."

The congresswoman regarded Jane carefully. "That's a very competitive award. I know from experience. Last year I served on the application review panel."

What incredible luck! Jane thought. This was the closest she'd ever been to an inside source on the McGill Fellowship selection process.

Congresswoman Kelso glanced down at her tidy desk. "I think somewhere in one of those piles was your résumé…"

"Oh, it's right here," Jane said, promptly locating the file.

The congresswoman studied it closely. "Want some unsolicited advice?" she asked.

Jane tried to contain her excitement. She wanted to jump up and down. "Of course."

"The panel is big on demonstrated leadership. Holding an office in student government carries a great deal of weight. Add that to your résumé, and you could stand toe-to-toe with any other applicant."

"What about extracurriculars?" Jane asked "I'm head cheerleader, captain of the debate team—"

"All good," the congresswoman cut in abruptly. "But not good enough. You're sharp, so I'll talk straight. You need to be class president," she said. "Trust me. I've been in that room when the applications are judged."

"But one of my best friends is running," Jane said. "It's Millie, actually."

The congresswoman shrugged. "My first political race was for a city council seat, and my opponent was a good friend. It's not the easiest thing in the world to deal with, but your reasons for running have nothing to do with your friendship and everything to do with serving your fellow students and pursuing your own goals. Don't be passive. Without the distinction of holding a class office, you won't make the first cut for the McGill Fellowship. It's that simple."

Jane's stomach did a death drop. She'd never expected to hear this. Everything in her life was planned from A to Z. Now she might have to squeeze in a student election! Against Derek Shafer, of all people, and one of her best friends!

"Ah, I see you uncovered the my-Satellites." The congresswoman picked up two electronic gadgets from her credenza. They were identical to the one that Tim had been using earlier.

Jane worked fast to pull herself together. She could have a meltdown later. "I saw Tim with one of those too. I've never seen these before."

"It's a new product being launched this season. My husband's a sales executive with the company. It got rave reviews at the last electronics show."

Jane took a closer look, playing with the buttons, checking out the features. The device had it all: appointment calendar, email, mobile phone, address directory, text messaging. "Wow. This thing can do everything."

"You're welcome to one, if you'd like," the congresswoman said.

Jane looked up. "Are you serious?"

"Why not? I've got two collecting dust, and I don't even know how to use the thing. Never had the time to figure it out."

Jane thought about it. Everybody seemed to be going towards digital day planners these days. In fact, her paper version seemed like something out of another century compared to this new device.

Suddenly a great idea flashed into Jane's mind. "You know, maybe I could transfer all your information to the my-Satellite. I'd like to do the same with my day planner. Then I could you show you how it works."

"Sounds great. I like your initiative. But I have to tell you I'm pretty inept when it comes to electronics," Kelso admitted.

Jane grinned. "Trust me. If I can teach my father how to use a universal remote control, I'll have you mastering the my-Satellite in no time."

The congresswoman laughed.

"Can you live without your day planner until tomorrow?" Jane asked.

Kelso shrugged. "Sure. My assistant knows more about my life than I do anyway."

Just then, Tim came running in to announce that the White House chief of staff was on hold for the congresswoman, and Kelso went straight for her phone.

Tim gave Jane a sharp look. "There's a mailing to get out."

"Yes, of course," Jane said, worried that she had rubbed him up the wrong way. The last thing she needed to do was offend anyone on Congresswoman Kelso's staff.

She gathered up her new project and quickly marched out, finding Millie camped out at a worktable in the main reception area, stuffing tons of envelopes.

Jane sat down and started doing the same. "Are there really ten thousand of these?"

Millie sighed and rolled her eyes. "Hey, nobody said it would be glamorous, right?" She paused. "So tell me, what's the congresswoman like? You were in her office for so long!"

Jane looked at her. "She's tough. But she's nice at the same time. I like her."

"Me too." Millie nodded. "Did she say anything about me?"

Jane hesitated. "Well, I told her you were running for class president."

Millie's eyes widened. "What did she say?"

"She thought it was great... but she thinks I should run too." Jane's gaze stayed locked on Millie, waiting for her reaction.

"Really?" Millie said. She seemed calm.

"You know I've been working towards the McGill Fellowship, right?" Jane asked.

Millie nodded.

"Well, Congresswoman Kelso said that holding a class office is practically a requirement for making the first cut," Jane explained.

"Then I guess it's decided. You're going to run," Millie said.

Jane stopped stuffing envelopes. "But I don't want to compete with you. You're my friend. I was supposed to help with your campaign, not run against you," she said.

Millie began to stuff even faster. "I'm totally cool with it. I mean, I know how much you want that fellowship. And if being class president will help you get it, you can't *not* run."

Jane's spirits soared. Millie was a great friend. "Do you really mean it?"

"Of course!" Millie exclaimed.

Jane hugged her friend. "Oh, thank you!"

Millie started to laugh. "That's settled. Now keep stuffing. We've got at least nine thousand five hundred to go!"

Jane started to stuff faster and faster, her mind working at the same speed. She'd be at a disadvantage, getting into the race for class president this late. Millie's cookie gimmick would generate plenty of attention. And Derek Shafer already had his campaign going full tilt.

But Jane wouldn't let that stop her. If she was going to enter this race, she'd be in it to win!

All she needed was a plan...

3

Jane scanned her list of things to do on her brand-new my-Satellite.

DELIVER ELECTION FORM TO STUDENT GOVERNMENT ADVISOR.

Done.

Mrs. Hayman had been so proud and encouraging about her bid for president. Jane made a note to look into faculty endorsements.

DRAFT COMMUNICATIONS PLAN FOR CAMPAIGN.

Done.

Between that and uploading all of her own and Congresswoman Kelso's information onto the my-Satellites last night, she was running on two hours of sleep, tops.

DELIVER INTENT-TO-RUN NOTICE WITH CLASS ANNOUNCEMENTS.

Almost done.

Jane was seated at the microphone now, waiting

for the go signal from the principal, Dr. Paige. Finally he gave her a nod.

Jane cleared her throat then pressed a green button on the mike, which meant her voice was now being broadcast throughout the entire school. "Good morning, South Side High! This is Jane Ryan. First up, congratulations are in order for the junior varsity soccer team. Last night they won their game against Brick Street High. Way to go, guys. Open auditions for *Guys and Dolls* will be held in the auditorium immediately following the last bell today and tomorrow. And don't forget – study sessions for the next SAT will begin Saturday morning at nine o'clock and continue for five weeks. Also, I have one more announcement to make, which concerns me, actually. I'm running for class president. You'll be seeing and hearing a lot from me in the very near future, but until then, make a special note to yourself that says, 'Vote for Jane Ryan.' Okay, that's it. Make it a great day!"

Jane took her finger off the button and groaned, then turned to Dr. Paige. "Did that sound okay?" she asked him. "I'm not used to making announcements about myself."

He gave her a warm smile. "You'd better get used to it if you want to be class president."

Jane nodded. *True*, she thought, and she headed off to class.

Later in the day, Jane stopped Roxy in the hall.

"Hey, what did I sound like on the announcements this morning? Be honest."

"Do you really want my opinion? No matter how bad it is?" Roxy asked.

Jane grimaced, bracing herself for the worst. "Yes," she said.

"I have no idea," Roxy said. "I was late for homeroom again and completely missed the announcements."

"Roxy!" Jane exclaimed, frustrated. "You had me freaking out there for a minute!"

"I'm the mischievous one," Roxy said. "I thought you knew that."

Jane gave her a half smile, half glare. "At least tell me that people are talking about my running for president."

"No, they're really not," Roxy admitted with a shrug. "But don't get bent out of shape. Rules of Modesty is doing a CD signing at the Media Riot Superstore. And don't forget about the Derek and Faith breakup. That's what everybody's talking about. You can't compete with a busted romance *and* a rock band."

"But *some* of the students have to be concerned about school issues, don't they?" Jane said.

Just then Chad Jovi, a popular senior and one of Derek's good friends, walked by with some other guys. "Dude, Rules of Modesty rocks! Those guys are cool. I've got to get my CD signed. I don't care how long the line is."

"It's true," Jane said. "Nobody cares about school politics anymore. What has this world come to?" Jane felt that familiar tightness in her chest. Suddenly she found it difficult to breathe.

"Are you okay, Jane?" Roxy asked.

Jane steadied herself against the lockers, trying to calm herself. *Breathe…*

That's when Babette Hill, another cheerleader on the squad, rushed up to her. "Oh, my God! You're running for class prez! That is so great! I'm so psyched! What can I do to help? Can I put up a sign? Where are your signs? You should have, like, signs *everywhere*. There are no signs! Do you have a campaign manager? Obviously not. Because a campaign manager would totally have signs out on the day that you announce! This is so wrong! *I* will be your campaign manager!"

Jane's breathing became more laboured. She was hyperventilating. Or suffering a panic attack. Or experiencing the sudden onset of some kind of anxiety disorder. Or all three at the same time!

And Babette was still talking. "How much money is in your campaign fund? We need, like, *major* dollars," she said.

Jane shut her eyes for a moment. *Deep breaths… slow breaths…* But even in this state of semi-panic, she knew one thing for certain. No matter how bad things got, Babette could never be her campaign manager. The girl was way too intense – even for Jane!

"Babette," Roxy said. "I've got one word for you – *chill*. Can't you see that Jane is totally stressed out?"

Jane opened her eyes.

Babette was staring right at her. "Do you need to, like, breathe into a paper bag or something?"

"No," Jane said. "I'm actually feeling better now."

"Your face has no colour," Babette went on. "Want to borrow some of my blush?"

"I'm fine," Jane assured her. "Really. And thanks for the offer. I'll need lots of help, but I've got the campaign manager part covered."

Babette pursed her lips into a baby pout. "Okay. But let me know if you change your mind." Then she moved on.

Roxy breathed a sigh of relief. "She's the one on top of the cheerleader pyramid, right?"

Jane nodded.

"And how many times has she fallen on her head?" Roxy asked.

"Don't be mean," Jane said. Then she let out a deep sigh. "I've got twenty million things to do for the election – that's on top of everything else I'm involved in."

"Well, at least you don't have to worry about the distraction of a boyfriend," Roxy put in. "Since you don't have one."

Jane shot a look at her sister. "Thanks for reminding me."

"Any time," Roxy grinned. "What else can I do to help? Seriously. I would much rather help than try to live with you when you're under huge amounts of stress. I *know* what that's like."

Jane started to take offence when her my-Satellite rang to the tune of ABBA's "Dancing Queen." It was her first call on the my-Satellite! She was so excited. "Hello?"

"It's Millie. Where are you?"

"At my locker with Roxy," Jane answered.

"I'm in the gym handing out cookies to athletes who will probably vote for Derek anyway," Millie said. "How stupid am I?"

"Hey, you never know," Jane said, trying to be encouraging. After all, she might need a pep talk herself soon. Going up against Derek Shafer was *not* going to be easy.

"Have you ordered any campaign material?" Millie asked.

"Not yet," Jane said. "I just finished my communications plan."

"Great," Millie said. "I know an awesome printing company. Street Smart Graphics. Ask for

Jeremy. They work fast, and their prices are really cheap. I got bids from several places, and Street Smart came in the lowest. If you put in an order now, they should have a proof ready late this afternoon and be able to deliver tomorrow. They are *so* fast."

"Thanks," Jane said. "That will save me some time. I'll see you in the parking lot after the last bell." She hung up.

Roxy was tapping one foot impatiently. "Any day now."

"What?" Jane asked.

"Hel-*lo*? I'm waiting for my first campaign assignment," Roxy replied. "Do you want me to write a speech, dig up a scandal on one of your opponents? Tell me."

"Wait!" Jane said, feeling a little overwhelmed again. She checked her schedule on the my-Satellite. How was she going to work at Kelso's office this afternoon *and* proof her order at Street Smart Graphics at the same time? She was a true control freak at heart and hated to turn over anything to anyone, but a girl could not be in two places at the same time. She glanced at Roxy. Her sister was a magnet for trouble. Could she handle this without somehow messing it up? "Okay, I've got a very important job for you."

Suddenly Jane sensed a strange vibe in the corridor. She turned to see two girls whispering and giggling by a notice board outside the principal's office.

Another girl yelled across the hall to her friend, "Heather, here he comes!"

Jane knew that all this could mean only one thing: a Derek Shafer sighting. She spun to see him walking down the hall smiling, eyes twinkling... at her? Yes! He was heading straight towards her.

She grabbed Roxy's arm. "Do I have lipstick on my teeth?" she asked.

"No, but you might want to think about introducing yourself to a TicTac."

"Oh, my God!" Jane exclaimed, completely mortified. She breathed into one hand to see if her sister was right.

Roxy laughed. "Relax. I was just kidding."

"I don't care," Jane whispered, fluffing out her hair a little. "Derek is heading this way. Give me a breath mint. Quick!"

"You have gone completely insane," Roxy said, fetching a tin of cinnamon mints from her backpack. "This time I'm *not* kidding."

Jane popped a mint into her mouth. "Okay, please go. If I say something stupid, I don't want to be reminded," she said.

"Whatever you say," Roxy replied, turning to leave.

"No, wait! Don't go!" Jane said. "The proof! The place is called Street Smart Graphics. Ask for Jeremy. My slogan is 'GO JANE RYAN!' All capital letters with a comma after 'GO' and an exclamation point at the end. Don't add anything else. I'm going for simple sophistication, not a Clash poster. Got it?"

Roxy nodded.

Jane gave her sister a little push just as Derek approached.

"I guess we're rivals now," he said to her.

Jane tried to be cool. "Friendly ones, I hope." She smiled.

"Oh, of course," Derek said. "I think it's great. But you've got me a little worried already."

"Please," Jane said. "I'll be lucky to get my own sister's vote."

Derek laughed. "Come on. Everybody knows that once Jane Ryan sets her mind on something… "

"Now who's being modest?" Jane asked. "You're, like, Mr. Popularity."

Derek laughed again. And he had the cutest laugh. "I don't know about that. But maybe I'll get the sympathy vote. You know, since Faith dumped me for a college dude."

At first Jane didn't know what to say. "Yeah, I heard. I'm sorry about that."

Derek shrugged. "Thanks. But it's no big deal. She wasn't the right girl for me."

Jane's mind was racing a thousand miles a minute as he spoke. *How could Faith dump him? He's so cute and smart and sweet and… uh-oh…*

At that very moment Jane noticed an awful sense of doom rising up within her. It was just hours into the election, and already her campaign was in serious trouble. How could she expect the majority of the school to vote for her instead of Derek?

Even *Jane* wanted to vote for him!

4

"The troops have arrived!" Tim shouted later that day. He intercepted Jane and Millie as soon as they walked into Congresswoman Kelso's re-election headquarters and pushed a huge stack of RE-ELECT KATE KELSO signs into Millie's arms. "We need these on every corner within a ten-block radius of this office, okay?"

"Absolutely," Jane said, moving to help Millie with the load.

"That job's for Melinda," Tim said. "The congresswoman wants to see you in her office."

Jane could see the frustration on Millie's face. "Mr. Goldsmith, her name is *Millie*, not *Melinda*," Jane said.

"I'm sorry, Janice. I won't make that mistake again," Tim said. And then he took off.

Millie rolled her eyes.

Jane grinned at Millie. "It's a good thing *he's* not running for office. Stay close by," she told her. "I'll come help you with those signs as soon as I'm done."

Jane made a beeline for Kate Kelso's office and found the congresswoman seated behind her desk, which was a mess compared to how Jane had left it yesterday but still not the disaster it had been before she worked her magic.

"Jane!" the congresswoman exclaimed. "I'm so glad you're here. You have no idea how excited my husband is that I'm going to be using the my-Satellite. How did the setup go?"

"Easier than I thought," Jane said.

"I need to be practising a speech for tonight, but I've got five minutes. Can you give me a crash course?" Kelso asked.

As if the congresswoman had to ask! Jane wanted to scream *Yes!* at the top of her lungs, but she didn't. No way.

"I'd be happy to," Jane told her. She reached into her backpack to retrieve the congresswoman's my-Satellite and her own, and the two sat on a couch by the window. "It's really a great little device. Very efficient. Follow along with me. I'll take you through all the bells and whistles."

"So everything that was in my day planner is in this little machine?" the congresswoman asked. "Every phone number and reminder?"

"Yes," Jane assured her. "Trust me. It's all there. Even your nephew's birthday. I set an alarm for one week prior to give you plenty of time to shop for a gift."

The congresswoman laughed. "That's good. Because last year he got his present a month late," she admitted.

"Every feature can be jumpstarted by pressing one of the icon buttons. The symbols are self-explanatory. We've got a calendar, address book, To Do list, email, mobile phone, and direct text messaging. That last one is really cool because you can beam live instant messages to any other my-Satellite user. Like your husband, for example. Or Tim."

The congresswoman smiled. "Or you."

Jane grinned. "That's right. Once you select a particular icon, an electronic tutor will take you through every function step-by-step. There's no way you can mess up. The tutor won't let you. As soon as you feel comfortable using the device without the tutor, just let me know. I can switch off the feature, and you'll move through the functions much faster on your own."

"What about cellular service?" the congresswoman asked.

"Already set up," Jane said. "I arranged for billing to go directly to your business manager."

The congresswoman shook her head in disbelief. "You're amazing, Jane. Between yesterday and today you've really made a difference in this office."

"Thanks. I just want to do a good job while I'm here," Jane said.

"You're doing a *great* job. And it won't go unnoticed. The high school internship programme is short. I realise you're only here for a few weeks. But if you ever need some help – a letter of recommendation, advice, anything – I want you to call me."

Jane was ecstatic! "Well, I'll let you get back to your speech. I should be helping Millie get those signs up."

The congresswoman stood. "Hey, I've got a signing for my new book at Barnes & Noble this weekend. I'd love for you to come."

Jane smiled. But instead of using her voice to answer, her fingers went to the my-Satellite instant text message feature. I'LL BE THERE! she typed, then clicked the send-message icon.

The congresswoman's my-Satellite beeped and vibrated. She pressed the correct icon, read Jane's message, and went through the motions of responding, a look of absolute delight on her face.

Now Jane's my-Satellite was vibrating. She read the screen. SEE YOU SATURDAY AT NOON! "Isn't it easy?" she said.

"It is easy," the congresswoman agreed. "Thanks to you."

Jane started for the door. "By the way, I didn't know you'd written a book."

"Hot off the presses," the congresswoman said. "I'll sign a copy for you on Saturday. It's called *Run to Win*. That's my personal motto for every campaign. Sounds simple enough, but you have to train your mind to think that way."

Jane nodded thoughtfully. *Run to Win*. That's exactly what she planned to do at South Side High. She couldn't wait until tomorrow. Getting her campaign materials would give her the chance to kick her run for class president into high gear. Plus, the pep rally for the junior varsity soccer team coming up on Friday would be a great place to make everybody remember three little words: GO JANE RYAN!

By noon the next day Jane was seriously freaking out, rushing to the main office between every class. This time Mrs. McCall, the principal's assistant, answered Jane's question before she could get so much as a word out.

"No, Jane, your package has not arrived yet."

Calm down. This is not a disaster situation. Yet, Jane thought.

She checked her task list on the my-Satellite. Jeremy from Street Smart Graphics had promised her delivery that morning. She had planned to inspect the first wave of campaign materials after first period. It was now the beginning of fourth period. She was *way* off schedule.

Jane clicked the phone icon on her my-Satellite. The number for Street Smart Graphics was stored in memory. She clicked on Dial. Jeremy had some serious explaining to do!

"Street Smart." It was him. She recognised his surfer dude voice immediately.

"Hello, this is Jane Ryan. I'm calling to check on the status of a delivery to South Side High."

"Yeah, sorry about that. Our driver's truck broke down this morning. He's running behind. But be cool. He'll be there soon."

Jane wanted to scream. *Be cool?* She was three hours off schedule, and he wanted her to be cool!

Deep breath, she told herself. She tried to be cool. It wasn't working. "Can you find out where the truck is now?"

Just then a muscular man in a STREET SMART GRAPHICS polo shirt stepped into the office wheeling three boxes behind him.

"Oh, thank God!" Jane exclaimed.

The delivery guy grinned and glanced down at his clipboard. "I take it you're Jane Ryan. Sign here, please."

Jane scribbled her signature.

"Where do you want these?" the driver asked.

"Right there is fine," Jane said, her eyes glued to

the boxes. Lunch would just have to be later. She couldn't wait to tear into them.

The my-Satellite started to ring to the tune of "Dancing Queen."

"Hello?" Jane answered.

"Where are you?" Millie asked. "We saved you a seat. And you'll never believe who's sitting at the end of our regular table – Derek. The whole breakup with Faith has totally shifted the usual lunchroom dynamics."

Jane looked up to see Mrs. McCall giving her a stern look. "I can't talk. I'm in the principal's office. My stuff from Street Smart showed up late."

"Okay," Millie said. "But hurry. Babette is giving me a headache. I need backup."

Jane hung up.

Mrs. McCall cleared her throat. "Jane, I'm sure you know the rule about mobile phone use during school hours."

Jane gave her a sheepish look. "Sorry."

Roxy stepped into the office. "Hey, what's up?"

Jane started to peel the packing tape off the first box. "My first bunch of campaign materials just came. How come you're not at lunch?"

"Not hungry. I chased down a protein smoothie before third period. Thought I'd work off a demerit during lunch hour. Want some help here?" Before waiting for an answer, Roxy ripped open another box, having much better luck than Jane. She held up a T-shirt. "Uh, the slogan is a bit off. Please don't freak."

Jane stared at the lettering in absolute horror. Instead of GO, JANE RYAN! the slogan read NO, JANE RYAN! "But you signed off on the proof! How could you let this happen?" Jane's voice came out as a shrill shriek.

"It's not my fault," Roxy said. "I could have sworn when I proofed it, it said *Go*, not *No*."

Frantically Jane tore through the boxes – baby tees, buttons, baseball caps, flyers, and banners. Everything was emblazoned with the phrase NO, JANE RYAN! "What am I going to do?" Then she turned to her sister. "Thanks a lot, Roxy."

"I can't believe it," Millie said two days later. "I've never had a problem with that company. The reason I suggested them is because they work so fast. I knew you wanted your stuff right away. I'm so sorry. This is awful."

"It's not your fault, Millie," Jane said. "Mistakes happen. Of course the timing on this one is about as bad as it can get." Miserably Jane watched as a group of seniors strutted by in Derek Shafer T-shirts.

The junior varsity soccer team pep rally was going strong, and the air crackled with excitement. It was Friday. Kids were ready for the weekend and Jane was ready for this event to be over.

She tried to make the best of it, mingling with other students, talking up her campaign promises, but without her jazzy advertising, it just wasn't the same.

Babette came running up to her wearing a Derek Shafer cap. "Oh, my God! Why did you drop out of the race? I'm totally depressed!"

"What are you talking about?" Jane asked. "I'm still in the race."

"But I haven't seen a single Jane Ryan cap, T-shirt, or anything," Babette said.

Humiliated, Jane pointed to one of her homemade posters.

"Oh," Babette muttered, obviously unimpressed. Slowly, she took off her Derek Shafer cap. "Okay, Jane, I'm totally behind you. I mean, like, one thousand percent. But that is a garage sale sign. You need to kick it up a notch."

Jane started to explain what had happened with the printing company, but then she stopped. What did it matter? She left Babette standing there and sat down on the bleachers.

All around her kids were whooping it up, cheering on the soccer team, sporting free campaign goodies, generally thrilled to be getting out of class one period early.

Jane felt as if her whole world was caving. How could she rebound from this? Even before today she'd been running behind. Right now the election seemed hopeless. And if the election was hopeless, then the McGill Fellowship would be harder to get. She had to figure out a way to make it *un*hopeless.

"Hey, it's supposed to be a pep rally. You don't look so peppy," Derek said, coming up to her.

Jane cracked a smile and half waved a finger in the air. "Yippee."

He sat down beside her. "Roxy told me what happened with the printer. That sucks. I'm sorry."

"I guess you can start writing your victory speech," Jane said.

"It's not over yet. You'll be tough to beat, even without signs and T-shirts. People at this school look up to you."

Jane glanced at him sceptically. "You're not just saying that?"

"It's true," Derek said.

Jane sighed, beginning to feel a little less sorry for herself. "I just feel like maybe I got into this race too late and that I'll never catch up."

Derek nudged her shoulder. "Want some free campaign advice? This is good stuff. I really should charge you for it."

Jane smiled. She couldn't believe how cute he was. "I'm listening."

"There's still time for two 'Cool Moves of the Week' before the vote. Make one of those, and you'll be a cinch to win."

Jane started to laugh. "Okay, I am *so* not a 'Cool Move of the Week' girl. That would be the other Ryan sister. She practically invented it."

"Hey, I think you're pretty cool," Derek said. "Doesn't that count?"

Before Jane could answer, Roxy interrupted them. "Hey, Derek, could you give me a minute with my sister? We need to have a private campaign strategy meeting."

"No problem," Derek said. "I'll see you later, Jane."

As soon as he walked away Roxy launched into a tirade. "Your campaign is in serious trouble. You just lost my vote, and I'm your sister!"

Jane gave her a stunned look. "Why?"

"Okay, student politics is not really my thing," Roxy continued to rant. "But removing all the vending machines from school property for health reasons? That's going too far. I've got to have my caffeine!"

Jane was truly confused. "Roxy, I have no idea what you're talking about."

"There's talk going around that dumping the vending machines is your big campaign issue," she said.

Jane couldn't believe it. "What? That's a total lie! I never said that!"

Roxy breathed a sigh of relief. "Good. But we've

got to clear this up. Even the slackers are ready to protest. And they don't get excited about anything but cool cars and hot parties."

Jane stood up. "Where did you hear about this?"

"From Teddy Somers," Roxy said.

"Great," Jane said. "That guy never even takes off his headphones, so it's obviously all over the school. The Jane Ryan campaign is cursed. It has to be!"

"Hey, look on the bright side," Roxy said. "Your campaign can't get any worse, right?"

My Scrapbook

5

"It's not NO, JANE RYAN! it's GO, JANE RYAN! One letter. Huge difference," Jane said. "*GO!* With a G. As in *green*. As in *gas*. As in *Google*. As in—"

"Yeah, we know what the letter *G* is," Jeremy said.

Jane bit her tongue. *I'm not so sure you do.* She wanted to say it, but she resisted. After all, she needed Street Smart Graphics to put a rush on this replacement order, and making them angry would not help the situation.

"I'm sorry about the mistake. I don't know what happened. I guess the dude in the back hit the wrong key or something. We'll have a new order delivered on Monday."

"Thanks, but please make sure it's right this time," Jane said before hanging up. She checked her Saturday-morning task list on the my-Satellite.

CALL STREET SMART GRAPHICS AGAIN.

Done. Even though she had gone over everything with them Thursday and Friday, it never hurt to reconfirm. She was a little worried about the fact that there was no time for a second proof, but no way could they mess up a simple three-word slogan twice. That would be too ridiculous.

Roxy appeared in the doorway of Jane's bedroom. "Guess what? I've got a great idea."

Jane narrowed her eyes at Roxy. Roxy's great ideas usually meant trouble.

"It's been a long time since we've just hung out and gone shopping. Why don't we take a trip to Summitt Village? Just you and me. Together. It'll be fun."

Jane narrowed her eyes. "We almost never do that."

"Then we should start," Roxy said. "Think of it as sister bonding time."

Jane knew there had to be some kind of angle. "What do you want, Roxy?"

Suddenly, Roxy's whole demeanor changed, revealing her con. "Okay, it's like this. Rules of Modesty is having an in-store signing at the Media Riot Superstore in Summitt Village. All my friends are grounded, and Dad has cleared me to go but only if you come with me."

"What did you do this time?" Jane asked.

"Two speeding tickets and five parking tickets. In one month. But none of them was my fault. Really."

Jane let out an involuntary groan. Her original

plan was to catch a ride with Millie straight to Congresswoman Kelso's book signing at Barnes & Noble. She was dressed for the occasion, wearing a pair of understated black trousers and a crepe top of the same colour. But Media Riot was just down the street from the bookstore…

"*Please?*" Roxy begged.

Jane relented. "Okay. But we can't stay long. I'm supposed to be at Barnes & Noble at noon for Congresswoman Kelso, and nothing can get in the way of that."

"Have I *ever* messed things up for you?" Roxy asked.

"Do you really want me to answer that?" Jane countered.

It took only twenty minutes to drive to Summitt Village, a new upscale outdoor shopping centre with a Media Riot Superstore, some clothing shops, a twenty-screen multiplex cinema, lots of cool restaurants, and a cyber coffee bar called High Speed Connection. Jane loved to hang out there with her friends.

"How's my makeup?" Roxy asked, checking her face in the rearview mirror. "Too much lipstick? I don't want to look like a groupie. I mean, I'm a musician. I want to look cool, but there's a fine line. You know?"

"Yeah," Jane said. "I know." But she was barely paying attention to Roxy. Her focus was the huge line of people outside Media Riot and the sea of cars in the parking lot. Talk about out of control. They'd never get out of here in time.

"Look, there's a spot," Roxy said, and she screeched into it. "Come on, Jane. Let's go!" She jumped out of the car to stake out a place in line.

With much less excitement, Jane followed.

A girl sidled up behind Jane causing her to do a double take. She was wearing the exact same jacket as Roxy – a vintage AC/DC satin tour number. Jane nudged her sister.

"Oh, my God!" Roxy squealed. "Where did you get yours?"

"Back Stage Door," the girl said. "It's not far from here."

"Me too!" Roxy cried.

Jane took out her my-Satellite to text message Congresswoman Kelso. GOOD LUCK WITH THE SIGNING. RUNNING LATE, BUT I'LL BE THERE.

A few seconds later a reply beeped in. I'LL SIGN ONE JUST FOR YOU.

"What's that?" Roxy's new friend asked.

"It's called a my-Satellite," Jane replied. "Mobile phone, scheduler, text messaging – basically like a Palm Pilot except it does everything."

"It looks cool," the girl said, peering over Jane's shoulder.

Jane gave her a look. It was totally rude to read someone else's text message!

The girl scowled then proceeded to ignore Jane and chat with Roxy. "What's your favourite Rules of Modesty song?"

"I like 'My Heart Is Bleeding,'" Roxy said. "Which guy in the band do you think is the hottest?"

Jane tuned them out as the line moved at a slow crawl.

Suddenly her my-Satellite jingled its "Dancing Queen" ring.

Roxy's new friend laughed. "Is that an ABBA song? How lame!"

Jane ignored her and answered the phone. "Hello?"

"I thought you'd be here already! The line is out of the door," Millie said over the phone.

Jane sighed. "I'm in another line, unfortunately."

"This is so cool," Millie said. "I've never had a book autographed before. Are you going to make it?"

Jane and Roxy inched their way towards the band. "I think so," Jane said. "Call me back once you get your book signed."

The line began to move at a faster clip. Now much closer to the band, Jane wondered what the big deal was. Their songs were pretty hot, but all the guys looked like they could use a good shower.

Finally Roxy's turn was up. She had the rock stars sign a small stack of CDs, posed for impromptu pictures with her digital cam, told them she was their biggest fan and a musician herself, and passed out her email address to each member. Finally the lovefest ended, and Roxy descended from the raised dais to pay for the CDs.

"Hurry," Jane said, grabbing her sister's arm as soon as the transaction was complete. "The congresswoman won't be at the bookstore much longer." Just as they reached the door, a major commotion broke out. A high-pitched alarm blared in three short bursts, and the crowd around Rules of Modesty lurched.

"What's going on?" Roxy asked. She started to head off in the direction of the chaos.

But Jane pulled Roxy through the exit door. "*Bookstore*. We're on a schedule."

"Oh, I forgot," Roxy grumbled. "I'm with the spontaneous party girl."

Jane ignored the dig and rushed to the car. As they drove away, a police car cruised up behind them and flashed its lights.

"Oh, my God!" Jane cried. "This cop wants you to pull over. Were you speeding?"

"Uh, hardly," Roxy said. "You would need your foot on the accelerator for that."

Roxy stopped the car and studied the police car in her rearview mirror. She saw a uniformed officer talking into his radio and staring straight at them. He pointed at her.

"Why is he pointing at me?" Roxy demanded. "I wasn't speeding!" She turned to Jane. "Sorry about this."

Jane looked at her watch. "Don't worry. We're not late... yet," she said.

"I just don't get it!" Roxy said. "We were barely out of the parking lot. How could they think I was speeding?"

The police officer proceeded to march towards their car, followed by another officer, who looked very young and very clumsy.

Jane just sat there, wondering what in the world could be happening.

"Excuse me," the officer said. "But I'm going to have to ask you girls to step out of the car."

"May I ask what this is about?" Jane said.

The second officer stepped up. "Don't make any sudden moves!" he blurted out.

The officer gave his partner a strange look. "Calm down, Prescott. I don't think these girls are going to make a run for it."

Prescott turned red, but stood tall. It must have been one of his very first days on the job. He looked a little jumpy.

Jane got out of the car first. "I'm sorry, Officer. Will you please tell me what this is about?"

Roxy jumped out next. "Yeah! I'd like to know too. I swear I wasn't speeding."

51

"Suspicion of shoplifting," the officer said.

Prescott pointed at Roxy. "Busted! Put your hands in the air!"

"Shoplifting?" Jane stared at her sister. When had Roxy start shoplifting?

6

"*Shoplifting*!" Roxy exclaimed. "Are you crazy?"

"Book her!" Prescott yelled.

"Book her for what?" the officer asked Prescott.

"Uh... insulting an officer? Oh... never mind," Prescott mumbled, turned red again and started to look a little shaky.

The officer tossed an odd glance in Prescott's direction.

"This is completely insane," Roxy fumed. "And what's this about shoplifting? I didn't steal anything!"

"We received a report that a young lady matching your description lifted a stack of CDs from the Media Riot Superstore. So please come back to the store with me to meet with security," the officer said.

Okay, Jane knew that her sister was a lot of things: allergic to homeroom, a night-owl, a girl who could never find her keys or keep her room tidy... but there was one thing that Roxy was not – and that was a thief!

Jane opened her mouth to speak.

But Roxy started on a rant. "Excuse me, but are you even aware of the sad state the music industry is in? Illegal downloads are killing CD sales. And stealing from retail stores? That's even worse! Why would I jeopardise the careers of my favourite bands? Hel-*lo*! If the money dries up in CD sales, they'll jack up the price of concert tickets. Have you any idea how much it costs to launch an arena tour? Trust me, you *don't* want to know. I plan to be a working musical artist myself one day, so why would I go around stealing from bands?"

The officer stared at Roxy with a frozen expression.

Finally Jane seized her moment to get a word in. "Roxy, why don't you just show them your credit card receipt for the CDs?"

"Oh," Roxy said. "Right." She fished out the receipt and thrust it into the officer's face. "*There*. Since when do shoplifters have receipts?"

The officer looked at the evidence and nodded. "Please accept my apology. You girls have a nice—"

"Wait a minute," Prescott said, moving in to inspect the receipt. He was trying very hard to prove himself, but doing a bad job of it. "This could be a counterfeit document she printed up to throw us off the scent!"

Roxy rolled her eyes. "Why did you think it was me in the first place?" she asked the police officer.

"A tip came in that the suspect was a teenage girl in an AC/DC tour jacket," he replied. "We were patrolling the shopping centre and Prescott here saw you getting into your car."

Instantly something clicked in Jane's mind. "Wait a minute. There was another girl in line with us wearing the exact same jacket!"

The officer stared accusingly at Prescott. "Another example of why rookies need better training courses. You had me tailing the wrong suspect."

Prescott turned red.

"She got away again," the officer said. "I've been after this shoplifter for months now. She's notorious. At the precinct we call her 'the klepto.'"

Roxy spoke up. "Uh, if we're talking about the same girl, her name's Shanna."

The policeman smiled politely and handed business cards to Jane and Roxy. "If you happen to see this Shanna again, call me at the precinct. I'm Officer Martin."

Jane gestured for Roxy to get into the car. *Please don't let it be too late. Please, please, please.* But by the time they arrived at Barnes & Noble, Congresswoman Kelso was long gone.

Jane saw Millie browsing in the magazine section and rushed over to her. "What time did she leave?"

Millie looked up from a fashion magazine. "A few minutes ago. What happened to you?"

Jane grimaced. "Long story. I thought you were going to call me."

"I did," Millie insisted. "I tried, like, five times and didn't get an answer. Then some girl picked up and told me I had the wrong number."

Alarmed, Jane dug into her backpack to fish out her my-Satellite. It wasn't there. "Oh, my God!"

"What's wrong?" Millie asked. "By the way, Jane, I don't know if I should tell you this or not, but Congresswoman Kelso seemed kind of annoyed that you didn't make it."

But Jane was barely listening. She slumped down onto a bench in front of the magazine rack and searched her backpack again. The my-Satellite was gone. "It's not here."

"What's not there?" Millie asked.

Roxy walked up to them, slurping a frozen smoothie. "I'm starving. Do you guys want to get some pizza?"

Jane took a deep breath and tried to remember the last time she had used the my-Satellite. Waiting in line at Media Riot. Suddenly a horrible reality hit Jane like a thunderbolt. Shanna, "the klepto"! The shoplifter from Media Riot! She had stood there in line practically drooling all over the my-Satellite. And now it was missing. Definitely not a coincidence. Deep down Jane knew that the girl had swiped it from her backpack.

"She stole it," Jane announced.

"Who?" Roxy asked. "And what did she steal?"

Millie gave Jane a concerned look. "Are you okay? You're really starting to act weird."

"Shanna – that girl the police are looking for." Jane glared at Roxy. "*Your* new best friend. She stole the my-Satellite from my backpack."

"Hey, don't put her with me," Roxy protested. "I was just trying to pass the time in line." She hesitated. "You really think she stole it? Maybe you left it somewhere. Maybe you should check the freezer when we get home."

Jane huffed. "I didn't *leave* it anywhere, Roxy! She stole it!"

Roxy shook her head. "That girl *is* a serious klepto," she said.

"I can't believe this!" Jane wailed. "The my-Satellite is gone. I missed the congresswoman's book signing. And for what?" She turned angrily to Roxy. "Just so you could get some stupid autographs!"

Roxy opened her mouth to speak but then apparently thought better of it.

"What am I going to do?" Jane asked. "Every-thing is in the my-Satellite. My phone numbers... my campaign schedule... my *life* schedule! I exfoliate three times a week. Did I last do it on Wednesday or Thursday? I can't remember! This could throw off my entire exfoliation process! Do you know how important exfoliation is for healthy skin? Do you have any *idea*?"

I should have known this would end up in disaster as soon as Roxy suggested hanging out together, Jane thought. *It was unnatural!*

Millie put a hand on Jane's shoulder. "It's going to be okay, Jane."

"Millie's right," Roxy said. "We'll find a way to get your gadget back, and until then you can just go back to using your nerd book."

"That's just it!" Jane wailed. "I threw it out! I was so excited about how great the my-Satellite was that I didn't think I'd ever need my day planner again!"

"Oh," Roxy mumbled, obviously at a loss for words.

And Jane didn't even want to *think* about having to explain this to Congresswoman Kelso. First she missed the book signing. Now she'd lost the my-Satellite. She could say goodbye to that letter of recommendation.

7

"I hope you did your reading, class," Mr. Oppen-heimer announced in English class on Monday, "because I'm giving you a quiz on the first fifty pages of Joseph Conrad's *Heart of Darkness*."

Jane buried her face in her hands. *Oh, God! That's why my alarm watch kept beeping!* All weekend she'd been writing bits and pieces of her life schedule and To Do lists in a notebook, but she'd forgotten about *Heart of Darkness*. She hadn't read a single page. How could she forget *Heart of Darkness*?

In a panic, she spun around to talk to Babette. "Quick. What's it about?"

"Are you telling me you didn't read it?" Babette asked. "But you *always* do the reading. Okay, this is weird. First the handmade posters and now this." She squinted at Jane. "You're not Jane Ryan. Who are you... really?"

Jane felt her anxiety rising. "Just give me something about the book! Anything!"

"It's about this guy..." Babette said.

Jane looked at her expectantly.

Babette shrugged. "That's pretty much all I got. It didn't make very much sense."

Jane turned back around to face the front of the class – and to face the reading quiz she would most certainly fail.

When the bell rang, Jane shuffled towards her next class in a daze. *The first F of my life*, she thought. *What kind of McGill Fellow fails an English quiz?*

Derek stopped her in the hall. "Earth to Jane."

She stopped, looked up at him, and smiled. "Sorry. I'm a million miles away."

"Sounds like a good place," Derek said. He held up *Heart of Darkness*. "I've got Oppenheimer next period."

Jane started to warn him about the quiz.

"Hey, did you get that mess worked out with the printing company? I haven't seen any of your posters yet."

Jane took in a sharp breath. Something *else* she'd forgotten! Street Smart Graphics was supposed to deliver today. "That reminds me. I have to go to the office. I'll talk to you later."

Jane did a fast walk to the office, waving at friends but not stopping. She had just enough time to check this out before her next class.

Suddenly Roxy fell into step right beside her and

removed the iPod headphones from her ears. "What's the hurry? Is there a fire I should know about?"

"Just stopping by the office to see if that printing company delivered what I paid for," Jane said, walking in to find three boxes from Street Smart Graphics on the floor. For a moment, she just stared.

"Well… aren't you going to open them?" Roxy asked.

Jane tensed up. "I can't do it. If it's wrong again, I don't know how I'll cope. You look first."

Roxy did the honours and pulled out a cute little T-shirt. "Brace yourself. It's still not right, but it's an improvement." She turned it around for Jane's benefit.

Jane gasped when she read the words on the tee. "YO, JANE RYAN!" she cried. "Why is this happening to me? What did I do?" She looked around. "Are there cameras on me? Is this some kind of sick reality show?"

"Sorry, Jane," Roxy said. "But this is your life."

Crouching down, Jane sifted through hundreds of tees, caps, buttons and flyers, each item defaced with the silly slogan YO, JANE RYAN! Then she gave the stash a second glance. "Where are the banners?"

Roxy looked too. "I don't know. They're not here."

Jane studied the delivery receipt Mrs. McCall had signed for on her behalf. "This says four boxes were delivered. I only see three."

Roxy asked other people working in the office,

but nobody had a clue about what had happened to the box with the banners.

Jane was now resigned to the fact that everything that could go wrong would go wrong. She had no choice but to roll with the punches.

"What are you going to do?" Roxy asked.

Jane reached down for one of the baseball caps and put it on her head. "What choice do I have? Students vote next week, and so far I'm the invisible candidate. I'm going to work it."

8

By lunch period Jane knew that YO, JANE RYAN! gear would be showing up on most of the student bodies. Jane, Roxy and Babette were set up right outside the cafeteria, handing out freebies to everyone coming in or going out.

"Yo, Jane Ryan!" kids shouted out from all directions. Finally! Her candidacy was getting some real attention. Hmm. Maybe the *YO* versus *GO* fiasco was a happy accident in disguise.

Derek came loping towards her in an exaggerated rap star walk and said, "Yo, Jane Ryan!"

Jane had to admit it wasn't the most original of jokes, but Derek looked really cute doing it. At first she laughed, but then she turned red with embarrassment, wondering if he might be making fun of her campaign.

"You've got the coolest slogan. Everybody thinks so. And you tried to tell me you're not a 'Cool Move of the Week' kind of girl. I wouldn't be surprised if you end up on the web and in the school newspaper this week."

Jane waved off his praise. "No way!"

Derek smiled, revealing sparkling white movie-star teeth. "I'd put money on it."

Jane laughed. "Well, I can't take credit for any of this. The printer made a mistake. It was supposed to say *Go*, Jane Ryan!"

Derek laughed too. "That's hilarious." He checked his watch. "Have you eaten lunch?"

Jane shook her head and gestured to Roxy, Babette, and the boxes of YO, JANE RYAN! stuff. "We've been at this the whole time."

He patted his backpack. "We can share mine." He glanced around. "I'm dying to get out of here for a bit. Let's go off campus to Zebra Park. I need some fresh air."

Jane's eyes widened, and she leaned in to whisper, "We can't just leave the school grounds. We'll get into trouble."

Derek gave her a confident nod. "I'll get us permission." His gaze shot over to Principal Paige, who always stood by to monitor lunch hour activities. Then he took Jane's hand. "Come with me."

Before Jane realised it, they were standing in front of the principal.

"Dr. Paige," Derek began, "Jane and I were wondering if we could have lunch off-campus today.

We need to take care of some last-minute campaign errands."

Principal Paige gave them both a critical look. "I suppose that's okay. You kids have been working hard. I'll sign you out with Mrs. McCall. Be back in time for fifth period. Otherwise you'll both face detention. Agreed?"

Derek nodded. "Thank you."

Jane nodded too. She waved goodbye to Roxy and Babette as Derek, laughing like a little boy, pulled her away.

"You didn't think I'd get away with that, did you?" he asked.

Jane felt swept away. It was a great feeling. Still, she had never done anything like this before. Skipping a class? That was Roxy's territory. "But what if somebody sees us?"

Derek acted as if he hadn't a care in the world. "Who cares? We've got permission now."

"Yeah, to do campaign errands," Jane pointed out. "Not go to the park."

Derek grabbed a flyer hanging halfway out of Jane's backpack. "We'll put this up on the park notice board. Satisfied?" He grinned.

Jane shook her head. "You're crazy."

They were in the student parking lot now, and Derek started walking backwards. "It's fun to do something a little crazy every now and then. Don't you think?"

Jane thought about it. Maybe he was right – because for her, this was definitely crazy, and it sure felt good.

"What's the last crazy thing you did?" Derek asked.

"My dad took me into Manhattan to see *Mamma Mia!* You know, the ABBA musical. 'Dancing Queen' is one of my all-time favourite songs. At the end of the show we danced in the aisle."

Derek grinned and laughed as he led her to his brand-new SUV.

"Nice car," Jane said as she hopped inside.

Derek gestured to a CD storage case on the floor near her feet. "Pick out some music. I just got the new Rules of Modesty. It's awesome."

Jane stiffened. "*Please*. Anything but that."

Derek laughed again. "What? You've got something against the band?"

"It's a long story," Jane said. She opened the case and began to scan the titles. "How about Syntax?" she asked. "They're pretty good."

"Sounds like a plan," Derek said. He slid the disc into the player.

Zebra Park was just minutes away from the school. The air was crisp, the sky was blue, and the sun was bright – an all-round perfect day to be in the park.

They found a clean picnic table, and Derek emptied

his brown bag to reveal his lunch: a peanut butter and jelly sandwich, a bag of crisps, a chocolate bar, and a juice box.

Jane giggled. "Do you always eat like a fourth-grader?"

"You laugh," Derek said, "but what you see here is fine cuisine. In my book this represents slaving over a hot stove."

Jane smiled. "Oh, really? Because I used to baby-sit a nine-year-old who could make her own grilled cheese sandwich."

"She must have been a mutant," Derek said with a serious look on his face.

Jane laughed. "She wasn't a mutant. I promise."

"So… are you having fun yet?" Derek asked.

"It started back there with Principal Paige," Jane answered. "And it hasn't stopped yet."

Without warning Derek leaned over and kissed her softly on the lips. "I've been wanting to do that for a long time. Now I can concentrate. So what were you saying?"

Shyly Jane turned away to take in a view of the trees. Her heart was beating fast, her knees practically shaking. *"I've been wanting to do that for a long time." What did that kiss mean?* She turned back to face him and started to laugh.

"What's so funny?" Derek asked.

"Nothing," Jane said. "I just can't believe this."

"What? That I've had a crush on you for months?" Derek said. "It's true."

For a moment Jane sat there, speechless. This was too good to be true. "But you hardly ever talked to me at school!"

Derek shrugged. "I'm a little shy when it comes to girls I like. It's the curse of all the men in the Shafer family."

Jane laughed. "I'd hardly describe your family as cursed. More like blessed."

Derek leaned back, and Jane noticed his muscular arms.

"Some blessings are a curse," he said. "There are certain expectations of Shafers. For instance, this election." He smiled at her.

Jane smiled back.

"Politics really isn't my thing, but my brother, my father and my grandfather have all held the office, so it's pretty much expected that I do the same. Ditto for college. Everybody went to Yale. Guess where I'm going?"

"Yale," Jane said.

"Bingo. What about you? Where are you going to college?" he asked.

"Well, I'm working hard towards securing the McGill Fellowship."

Derek whistled. "That's no joke."

Jane nodded seriously. "Tell me about it. But it

would give me a chance to attend college in England. Oxford, actually. That's always been a dream of mine."

"And to think some girls at South Side are just worried about who's going to ask them to the prom," Derek said.

"Hey, I'm worried about that, too. I may be an overachiever, but at the end of the day, I'm still a girl."

Derek smiled at her again.

Jane looked up at the beautiful sky. "I suppose we should be getting back. Otherwise it's detention, and the last thing the school needs is another Ryan sister in detention."

Derek laughed, stretching lazily as they stood. He started to walk back to the car then stopped. "This is our first date, right?"

Jane shrugged. "I guess."

"Then I'd better kiss you," Derek said.

Jane looked up at him. "You already did."

"That first one was just for practice." And then Derek planted an even softer kiss on her lips.

This time Jane gave in to the moment completely, putting her arms around his neck, feeling the butterflies take flight in her stomach. The kiss lasted for several long, delicious seconds. And it was the best kiss *ever*.

As they made their way back to the car, Jane wondered how any date could be this perfect.

Getting into the front passenger seat, her gaze fell to the back, where she noticed a box from Street Smart Graphics. Peering more closely, she saw her name on the side of the box. Those were her missing campaign banners! Why did he have them?

Derek looked back to figure out why she was staring. "Hey, what's your box doing in my truck?" Derek asked.

"I was about to ask you the same question," Jane snapped.

"I don't have any idea," Derek said.

"Why not? It's your car. How many people at South Side have the keys?" Jane asked.

"Jane, I'm serious – I don't know anything about that box."

As much as it hurt, Jane didn't believe him. How could she? Her campaign had been hit with all sorts of bad luck – the printing fiasco, the ugly rumour about the vending machines – while his was coasting along with no problems at all. It just didn't add up. "Is cheating part of the Shafer tradition too?" she asked.

Derek shook his head. "I'm not a cheater, Jane. I don't have to cheat."

Jane glanced at her box of banners again. *Give me a break*, she thought. The proof was sitting on his back seat. "Just take me back to school."

Derek hopped into the driver's seat and slammed the door. "Great idea," he said tightly.

Jane was silent the whole ride back. All she could think about was how much she wanted to beat him in the election. It would take more than a few kisses to turn her into a blind idiot. Derek Shafer might be a player, but he was about to get played. Only Jane planned to do it fair and square.

9

"He's a jerk," Roxy said the next morning. "No – hold that thought. *Jerk* is too nice a word for him. Derek Shafer is a sewer rat."

Jane sighed as they made their way into the front entrance of South Side High School the next morning. "Can we please talk about something else? The whole Derek-Shafer-is-a-pig thing is getting old. I kissed him once. Okay, twice. Whatever."

"But I need to vent," Roxy said. "I'm just hearing about this now."

"That's because you went out after school and missed curfew last night. Where were you?" Jane asked.

Roxy averted her eyes. "You know... I was... around."

Jane stopped in her tracks just in front of the principal's office. "Listen, I don't have time to drag the truth out of you this morning. I have to make the announcements."

She stepped into Principal Paige's office and went straight for the public address system.

He gave her the nod, and she did her thing. "Good morning, South Side High!" she said into the microphone. "This is Jane Ryan with a few newsworthy bulletins. Callback auditions for *Guys and Dolls* will be posted outside the auditorium after school today. Kudos to the golf team for advancing to the state finals. Look for yearbook sales to begin next week. And last but certainly not least, yours truly will be holding court outside the cafeteria during fourth period lunch today to answer any campaign questions and distribute platform literature. I hope to see you there. Make it a great day!"

Later in the day, just as Jane was getting settled at her campaign table, Millie approached and offered her a frosted cupcake with VOTE MILLIE spelled out in multicoloured sprinkles.

Jane took a bite right away. "This is delicious!" she said. "And all I've got for voters is this brochure. Take a look."

Millie picked up one of them and gave it a quick read. "When did you do this? It spells out your whole platform."

"Last night," Jane said. "I was still so mad about Derek that I couldn't sleep. So I got up and did some work. It's a quick photocopy job, but it makes my case."

"So it's true," Millie said. "I heard Roxy talking. I can't believe he stole your banners. That's really low."

Jane nodded as she killed off the rest of the cupcake.

A skater-boy type lurked around the table behind Millie.

"Oops," Millie said. "I'm blocking potential voters. I'll talk to you later. Remember, we're due back at Congresswoman Kelso's office today." She gave a little wave and shuffled down the hall.

The skater boy approached the table, a long fringe covering his eyes. "What's up?" he asked.

"Not much," Jane said. "Did you have a question about my platform?"

"Uh… not exactly. But Roxy's cool. Does she have a boyfriend?"

Jane gave him an annoyed look. "That's not really a campaign question. Why don't you ask *her* if she's dating anybody?"

"Some dude told me you would answer any question about Roxy at this table."

"Well, the *dude* misinformed you," Jane said. "I'm here to talk about my platform for senior class president."

"As president, can you help make Roxy my girlfriend?" the boy asked.

"No," Jane said, glancing around him. "Next!"

she called out.

The skater boy disappeared.

A girl with a hard look stepped forward and placed a CD on the table. "If I vote for you, will you get me backstage passes or whatever?"

Jane gave the girl a puzzled look. "What?"

"I figure since you're Roxy's sister, it wouldn't be that big of a deal."

Jane had a strong sense that there was more to this sudden interest in Roxy than just her sister's coolness factor.

Two students walked right past Jane's table on their way to the cafeteria. "It's the best 'Cool Move of the Week' ever," one girl said.

"Roxy Ryan is amazing. The girl totally rocks," the other girl added.

Jane remained at her station for another fifteen minutes, but every second was pure torture. Finally she left her table to find Roxy.

Passing by one of the computer labs, Jane noticed a group of kids crouched over a laptop.

From somewhere in the huddle came a shout. "Look! There's Roxy getting dunked by the Rules of Modesty drummer!"

Jane pushed her way to the front of the crowd so she could see what was going on.

"Wow! I don't believe it," another student exclaimed. "How did she get into a VIP pool party for Rules of Modesty?"

Jane, close enough to see the computer screen now, gasped in disbelief herself. There were about half a dozen digital images of Roxy partying with the rock band! And every image had been uploaded to South Side High's student-designed website. More importantly they were on the most popular page, "Cool Move of the Week."

"Check it out," a girl close to the front said. "Roxy's playing air guitar on the diving board. That girl rocks."

"I want to know how she got into that party," a guy at the back demanded. "My cousin works for a radio station, and he couldn't even get past the band's security."

"I heard that she bluffed her way in with a fake press badge that she made in graphic design class," a voice called out.

"Yeah," confirmed another. "That's what I heard too. She ditched the last two periods yesterday too. That truant officer guy didn't have a clue. The dude is a total idiot."

So this is why Roxy missed curfew last night! Jane said to herself. *My sister was partying with rock stars!*

Having seen enough, she pushed her way out of the huddle and stomped back to her table in front of the cafeteria. Visitors to her Q&A post were few and far between. As much as she hated to admit it, Derek was right. The way to get attention at South Side High was to make a cool move and end up on that website.

Jane's spirits sank. There would only be one more "Cool Move of the Week" posting before the election. What could she possibly do that would top Roxy's rock star party?

10

"We're calling to ask for your vote to re-elect Congresswoman Kate Kelso. Election day is November fifth," Jane said.

"Oh, I'm behind her all the way," the man said. "She's done great things for this area."

"I couldn't agree more," Jane said. "Thank you, sir." She hung up and looked at Millie wearily.

"Two people yelled at me because I called during their favourite TV show," Millie said. "I'd rather be pounding the pavement and putting up signs."

Jane sighed. "Working a phone bank is tough, but it's got to be done. Most people I've called have been nice, though."

"You must have the lucky list," Millie said.

Jane, having been at it for two hours straight, leaned back to take a five-minute break. She stole a glance at the congresswoman's office door. It had been closed all afternoon.

Millie leaned across the table to whisper. "Have

you talked to her since the book signing?" she asked.

Jane shook her head. "No."

"Maybe you should just leave it alone," Millie suggested. "Like I said, she was pretty mad at you that day."

But Jane couldn't leave it alone. She had to explain to the congresswoman that she'd had every intention of being there *and* confess that her my-Satellite had been stolen.

Abruptly Jane stood up. She hated avoiding issues or dreading the inevitable. Putting your cards on the table was the only way to live. She marched to the congresswoman's private office and knocked on the door.

"Come in," the congresswoman said.

Jane stepped inside.

Congresswoman Kelso sat behind her desk, reading glasses on the tip of her nose, going over a stack of papers. "Hi, Jane. I'm preparing for a legislative vote. Is this something that can wait?"

At first Jane felt compelled to back out of the room. But in the end she decided to stay. "Do you have two minutes?"

The congresswoman took off her reading glasses and softened a little. "Sure. I have two minutes. What's on your mind?"

"First, I owe you an apology for missing the book signing on Saturday. I got caught up in a problem with my twin sister."

The congresswoman broke out into a huge grin. "You're a twin? I didn't know that!"

Right away, Jane felt her nervousness disappear. "I had every intention—"

"Jane, you don't need to explain. I have a sister too. Families can complicate even the best-planned day. But we wouldn't have it any other way, would we?"

Jane grinned. "I guess not." She paused for a second. Now for the tough part. "There's something else. The my-Satellite you gave me… It was… it was stolen."

The congresswoman looked alarmed. "Stolen?"

Jane nodded. "From my backpack."

"Oh, Jane, that's terrible. I thought something strange was going on when I didn't hear back from you after my last few text messages."

"I should have called to tell you right away… but I was too embarrassed," Jane said.

"Why?" the congresswoman asked. "It's not your fault. You're the victim of a crime."

"It was the combination of everything. Millie mentioned that you were upset that I didn't make the book signing, and the last thing—"

"Millie said that?" the congresswoman cut in.

Jane nodded.

"Well, that's simply not true. Your name never even came up at the book signing."

For a moment Jane just stood there, completely stunned. Why would Millie lie about something like that?

An elderly volunteer stepped into the doorway. "Jane, there's a call for you on line three, sweetie."

Jane smiled at the congresswoman. "I should let you get back to work, anyway."

"Don't worry about the book signing," the congresswoman said. "But there *is* a way you can make it up to me."

Jane smiled. "Just name it."

"Come to my book party the day after tomorrow. It's at the Durkin Hotel from five to seven."

"It would be an honour!" Jane said, excited.

"Excellent," the congresswoman said. "I'll have Tim add your name to the guest list. Oh, and, Jane, don't mention this to Millie. This is a special invitation just for you. I have something else in mind for her."

Jane nodded and stepped out of the office, closing the door behind her. She watched Millie working the phones and wondered again why her friend had told that lie. Maybe Millie was jealous of the way Jane and the congresswoman got along.

Suddenly Jane remembered her phone call and raced to an empty desk to pick up. "Hello?"

"Jane, it's Derek. Listen, before you—"

"Derek, I have nothing to say to you. And please

don't call me at work. It doesn't look good for me to receive personal calls here." Then she hung up. But as much as she tried to pretend that she was over him, it still hurt to hear his voice.

The next morning at school Jane knew that getting rid of Derek would not be so easy... because he was waiting at her locker.

Jane ignored him, retrieving her French workbook and slamming her locker door shut. She tried to move around him, but he blocked her path.

"At least give me a simple good morning." He smiled that amazing smile.

Jane wanted to smile back, but she held firm. "Please get out of my way."

"Not until you hear me out," Derek said.

Jane crossed her arms defiantly. "Make it quick. I don't want to be late for class."

"I have no idea how those banners ended up in my SUV. All I know is that I didn't have anything to do with it. You have to trust me, Jane. If I was lying about it, don't you think I'd come up with a better explanation than 'I don't know'? And don't you think I would have hidden them in the boot, so you wouldn't see them?"

Jane could feel herself softening a little. He did have a point.

"This election isn't even that important to me,"

Derek went on. "I'm doing it more out of obligation and family expectations than anything. But if going ahead with it means that we can't be friends, then I'll drop out of the race today."

Jane stared at him, stunned speechless. This wasn't a line. Derek meant every word. She could read the honesty in his eyes. "Don't drop out because of me," she said.

"I don't have any business running, anyway," Derek said. "I saw the brochure you made. That took time and real effort. I haven't done anything like that. I'm just running on popularity."

Jane shook her head. "You're a leader, Derek. Other kids look up to you. I'll feel terrible if you drop out of the race."

Derek hesitated. "So kids look up to me, huh?"

"Of course they do!" Jane said.

"Well, right now I feel like someone's out to get me. Somebody put your banners into my car. I just wish I could find out who."

Jane shrugged. "I don't know, but the election is next week. Let's just hope the worst is behind us."

Derek smiled. "Does this mean I have a shot at a second date?"

Jane reached into her backpack and pulled out a YO, JANE RYAN! cap. "*If* you wear one of these."

Derek immediately stuck it onto his head. "How about Saturday?"

Jane giggled, taking in the YO, JANE RYAN! hat with the DEREK FOR PREZ – THE ONLY WAY TO VOTE T-shirt. "You look like a guy who can't decide."

"Oh, I know what I want," Derek said. "You can count on that."

Jane felt a blush warm her cheeks.

"Hey, Derek!" a voice shouted from down the hall.

Jane turned to see Derek's friend Kirby Reynolds hanging halfway out of the library door. "Have you seen the 'Cool Move of the Week' yet? Come check this out!"

Jane let out a low groan.

"Don't get too bent out of shape," Derek said. "Next week there'll be a new 'Cool Move,' and this one will be forgotten. Who knows? Next week maybe it'll be you."

"For what – speed reading?" Jane cracked. "Believe me, it's not going to happen." She followed him into the library, and they joined a group of his guy friends checking out the South Side site on one of the Internet monitors.

"This girl is mad crazy," Kirby was saying. "I can't believe she conned herself into that party."

"She's pretty hot too," a soccer player named Will remarked.

Derek popped Will on the head.

Will glanced back, caught sight of Jane, and laughed out of embarrassment.

"That's my sister," Jane said.

"Oh… um… yeah," Will stammered. "But since you're twins… I guess you're pretty hot too."

Derek popped Will again.

Kirby shook his head. "Dude, what'd I tell you about doing too many head-butts on the field?" he said to Will.

Everybody laughed.

Jane turned her attention back to the computer monitor. One of the digital snapshots captured her curiosity. It was Roxy being dunked in the pool by one of the Rules of Modesty band members. But Jane was struck not by that but by the sight of a girl lounging on a chaise in the background.

Leaning in closer to the screen, Jane pointed at the image. "Can you make that bigger?"

Kirby navigated the mouse, did a quick double click, and the girl's image ballooned to fill the screen.

Jane gasped, recognising her immediately. "It's her!"

"Who?" Derek asked.

"The girl who stole my planner!" Jane screamed.

11

As soon as Roxy got home from detention that afternoon, Jane took her straight to her laptop computer. "Look!"

"Kindly remove your finger from the middle of the screen, and I will," Roxy said.

Jane took a step back.

Roxy peered more closely. "That's 'the klepto'!" She turned back to Jane. "I can't believe we were at the same party, and I never even saw her. Isn't that crazy?"

Jane glared. "Yeah, it's wicked wild." She rolled her eyes. "That thief has the my-Satellite, and I want it back. So what's the plan?"

Roxy drew back in shock. "You're asking *me* for help?"

"You know what they say. Desperate times call for desperate measures."

Roxy zeroed in on the digital image of "the klepto," concentrating as if the subject were hard science.

"I'm trying to put myself into her head," she explained. "You know, figure out what makes her tick. Now if I were a klepto, where would I be?"

Suddenly Roxy's fingers flew across her laptop's keyboard, bringing up her email page. She opened a message. "I just got an invitation from Back Stage Door to preview a new shipment of vintage rock tees before they put them on the racks for the masses." She read the message again. "It's set for tomorrow afternoon."

Jane didn't get the connection. "So?"

"*So*, chances are 'the klepto' got this email too. We both bought our AC/DC jackets at Back Stage Door. Listen, the girl will be there with bells on. Vintage T-shirt fans are a choosy bunch. And good stuff from the eighties flies out of stores as fast as it comes in. Going to a preview is the difference between scoring a cool Motley Crue tee or ending up with a cheesy Rick Springfield tank top. Trust me. She'll be there."

What Roxy was saying seemed to make sense – granted, in a very Roxy way. "Maybe it's not such a long shot," Jane said.

"We should go," Roxy said.

Jane started to agree, then grimaced. "I'm supposed to be at the Durkin tomorrow. Congress-woman Kelso is having a book party, and I can't miss that like I missed her signing."

Roxy waved a dismissive hand. "Whatever! The preview starts at three. You'll have plenty of time to get there. Do you want your my-Satellite back or not?"

"I do," Jane said, nodding. "Let's go for it."

The following afternoon Jane was dressed to kill in a smart designer suit that gave off serious Washington lobbyist vibes. Roxy was dressed to thrash in distressed jeans and a vintage Ramones T-shirt.

"I'm sick of this," Jane whispered. "We've been in this stinky place forever." She glanced around the musty shop. Why did Roxy think this store was so great, anyway? It was basically a tiny space full of old, dirty clothes. "And how long can I pretend to shop?" she went on. "The girl behind the counter is looking at me like *I'm* a shoplifter!"

"Just relax," Roxy whispered. "Stakeouts take time. This isn't a cop show where everything wraps up in an hour."

For the millionth time Jane browsed through a rack of concert tees.

Suddenly Roxy sidled up beside her and talked out of a corner of her mouth. "She's here. But don't look up. Stay very calm. Let her pick out some clothes, and we'll nab her when she comes out of the dressing room."

Jane struggled to keep her cool. She wanted to

tackle the girl and wrestle her down for the my-Satellite!

Shanna made a few selections, then disappeared into the dressing room. In a flash she was out, twisting and turning in front of the full-length mirror to check the look and fit of an early Bon Jovi number.

In the reflection Jane made solid eye contact with "the klepto."

Smugly the girl put on a show of ignoring her.

Jane held her ground, furious that this petty thief would even try such a stunt. "Excuse me," she said boldly. "You can pretend all you want, but you have something that belongs to me. I suggest that you hand it over."

Shanna barely raised an eyebrow. Then she stepped towards Jane, invading her personal space. "I suggest that *you* get a life. I don't have anything of yours. Do I even know you?"

"Nice try," Jane countered. "But we had the misfortune of meeting at Media Riot."

Shanna shrugged and turned back to face the mirror. "You must have me confused with someone else. I've never been there."

Suddenly Shanna's backpack began to ring to the tune of ABBA's "Dancing Queen"!

Jane spun around.

Roxy was on her cell phone, calling Jane's my-

Satellite number, punching the air with a victory fist.

"Funny," Jane said. "You don't look like an ABBA fan."

Shanna gasped. Then she took off like a bullet.

Jane was shocked by how fast the girl could move. No wonder she'd never been caught! "Roxy, stop her!"

Even though Roxy was closer to the exit, Shanna bolted so fast that she got an easy head start.

Jane followed Roxy, and just as she sprinted out of the store, she could hear the manager yelling into the phone, "I want to report a shoplifter!"

Jane trailed after Roxy and "the klepto," panting all the way. "Get her, Roxy! Get her!" Then she spotted a police car following them, lights flashing and siren blowing. "Roxy!" she called out breathlessly.

Roxy turned back and saw the car right away.

The car turned the corner at high speed and screeched to a halt in front of them. Officer Martin and Prescott the Rookie jumped out.

Jane frantically pointed in the direction of Shanna, who was still running and leaving all of them in the dust. "She's getting away!"

But Officer Martin ran towards Jane and Roxy, intercepting them within moments and stopping them from going after Shanna. "Hold it right there, girls."

Jane stopped short and tried to catch her breath. Once more she pointed in the direction of "the klepto" for emphasis. "Wrong girl… getting away… shoplifter."

Roxy was in worse shape than Jane and couldn't even get out that much. She just remained doubled over, gasping for air.

"Martin, should I close off this street?" Prescott asked. "This could be a dangerous situation. We don't want any civilians injured."

"The shoplifter is getting away!" Jane gasped.

Prescott pointed at Roxy. "No, the shoplifter has been caught!"

"I… didn't… take… anything!" Roxy wheezed.

"Anything you say can and will be used against you—" Prescott said quickly without listening to a word that Jane and Roxy were trying to tell him.

Officer Martin shook his head. "Prescott, don't get carried away."

"We were chasing 'the klepto'! She was right in front of us" Jane said, still catching her breath.

"So you're saying you're not the shoplifters," Prescott said with a feeble swagger.

"No!" Jane shouted. "Every time we turn around, you're accusing us of stealing! Meanwhile the real thief continues to get away. The same thief who stole the my-Satellite that was given to me by Congresswoman Kate Kelso!"

Officer Martin regarded her carefully, and Jane could tell that the mere mention of the congresswoman's name carried major weight.

"Seriously, we were chasing after the real shoplifter, but you stopped us," Roxy said. "The girl who stole the CDs at Media Riot. She was right in front of us!"

Officer Martin looked at Roxy, but didn't seem convinced. "I'm sorry, girls, but two incidents in a row is suspicious. I'm going to have to take you in."

"Let's cuff 'em." Prescott added dramatically, still turning his usual shade of red.

Just then, the manager from Back Stage Door came running down the sidewalk. She looked at Officer Martin and Prescott, then turned to Roxy. "Did you catch the shoplifter?"

Prescott stepped forward, puffing out his chest. "The shoplifter is right here," he said, pointing to Roxy.

The manager gave him a strange look. "What are you talking about? She's one of my best customers!"

Roxy smiled proudly.

Officer Martin hung his head, sighed, and then nodded at Jane and Roxy. "Alright, girls. It looks like you just keep ending up at the wrong place at the wrong time. You can go."

Jane glanced at her watch and practically yelped when she saw the time. Congresswoman Kelso's book party had already started. But if she left right now, she just might make it...

12

Jane finger-combed her hair, smoothed the skirt of her pale pink suit, and prepared to enter the Durkin Hotel to attend her very first book party.

She met up with a sea of impressive men and women, all of them older, established and successful. Suddenly Jane felt like a little girl playing dress up. What was she doing here?

She saw a familiar face in a small crowd across the room – Millie. Jane waved excitedly, but Millie didn't look so happy.

As the cluster of partygoers broke apart, Jane realised why. Millie was wheeling a cart of hot hors d'oeuvres, steam rising up from the food straight into her face.

Jane rushed over. "You look swamped. Can I do anything to help?"

Millie shrugged. "The caterer was shorthanded, but I've got it covered. Thanks." She pushed the cart towards a group of businessmen.

Jane scanned the crowd for anyone from Kate Kelso's campaign office. She spotted a few volunteers, but they were all engaged in conversations.

At that moment Jane would have gladly traded places with Millie. At least Millie had something to do. *Stop it, Jane*, she told herself. *Congresswoman Kelso invited you. Why should you feel uncomfortable at this party just because you're young?*

Feeling a surge of confidence, Jane boldly approached a small group talking politics and attempted to join them.

"So then this joker tries to sell me on sending him to a teen marketing seminar. Can you believe that? He wanted to waste fifteen hundred dollars of the company's money. I told him to forget it."

Others in the group nodded in vague agreement.

But Jane spoke up. "There are thirty-two million teenagers in America, and they spend about ninety-five billion dollars a year. I'm not sure you want to ignore that market."

All eyes zeroed in on Jane.

"What's that, little girl?" the businessman asked, his voice patronising. He laughed a little and threw back a swallow of his drink.

"I'm a senior in high school," Jane countered. "Hardly a *little girl*."

"You're no CEO, either," the man said, laughing again, more to the group than to her.

There were a few snickers.

"I know kids like you contribute to the economy," the man continued. "But it's mostly by buying movie tickets and fast food. I sell expensive electronics, sweetheart. If I want to sell to you, I'll advertise to your daddy."

Jane shook her head. "Actually, the fact is that teens make their *own* buying decisions. We get money as gifts. We have part-time jobs. We draw allowances from our parents. That can add up to a lot of money. And we know how to save it to buy the mobile phones, video games and digital cameras we want."

There was a whistle of appreciation for Jane's argument, and a larger crowd began to gather, including Congresswoman Kelso.

"What does a girl like you know about business anyway?" the man challenged.

"I know enough to realise that fifteen hundred dollars for a teen marketing seminar would probably be the best money you ever spent. Teens have a major amount of expendable income. Most focus groups, marketing efforts and advertising plans are geared toward getting a piece of it."

Congresswoman Kate Kelso smiled. "Nicely done," she praised, taking Jane off to one side. "You made some great points there. I'm sure your classmates would appreciate how you stuck up for them."

Jane noticed Millie making another round with the pushcart. "Should I be helping Millie?"

The congresswoman smiled tightly. "No, you should be watching out for her. I'm not sure Millie has your best interests at heart."

Later that evening Jane was staring at the ceiling in her bedroom, thinking hard on what Congresswoman Kelso had said about Millie.

The telephone rang, and Jane answered to find Derek on the other end. Her heart soared at the sound of his voice.

"Hey, I've got some not-so-great news," he said, sounding bummed.

"What's wrong?" Jane asked.

"More campaign trouble," Derek said.

Jane couldn't believe it. "Now what?"

"This time you've got some company for your misery," he said. "They hit both of us. Some of our banners have spray paint all over them – but most of them were just ripped right off the school's walls. They're gone."

"This is getting out of hand," Jane said.

"I know," Derek agreed. "We've got to find out who's doing this!"

"I think I've got a pretty good idea," Jane said.

"Who?" Derek demanded.

Jane paused. She didn't want to admit this, but

after what the congresswoman had told her, she had to. "I think it's Millie."

"Millie?" Derek exclaimed. "But she's your good friend!"

"Maybe not as good as I thought," Jane said. "Isn't it funny that nothing's happened to Millie's campaign?"

"Yeah," Derek said. "That is weird."

Everything started to make sense. After all, it was Millie who'd strongly recommended Street Smart Graphics, the company that couldn't get anything right. She probably started the vending machine rumour and stole the banners too!

"But why would Millie do it?" Derek asked. "Just to win the election?"

"I don't know," Jane said. "Maybe she got mad when I decided to run. Or maybe she was jealous because Congresswoman Kelso likes me so much. Who knows?"

"'Who knows' is right," Derek pointed out. "We still don't know for sure if she did it."

"You're right," Jane said. "But I'm going to find out." She signed off with Derek and went straight to the person who she knew could help her get to the bottom of this mess – Roxy.

The only problem with asking for Roxy's help was doing thing's Roxy's way...

• • •

Wearing solid black workout suits, Jane and Roxy ventured out into the night, driving to Stone Water Bend, a gated community about ten minutes away, where Millie McDonnell lived.

Roxy parked in front of a darkened house in a cul-de-sac and tried on her night-vision goggles for size. "Love The Sharper Image. I knew these would come in handy one day."

"So what are the raw eggs for?" Jane asked, pointing to the ones in the front pockets of Roxy's zippered hoodie.

Roxy shrugged. "Revenge." She strapped her digital camera around her wrist and checked the battery charge level. "Plenty of juice," she said. "Let's roll."

They proceeded to Millie's address on foot.

Jane was a nervous wreck. "This is crazy. I can't believe I let you talk me into this."

"You want to know the truth, don't you?" Roxy whispered. "There's only one way to find out. You can't just walk up to Millie and say, 'Excuse me, have you been plotting against me all this time like some evil villain?'"

Jane laughed a little. "No, I can't do that."

"That's her house up ahead," Roxy said. She ran to check out the situation and then waved for Jane to hurry up.

Jane picked up her pace.

THE SECRET OF JANE'S SUCCESS

"I think there's a light on in the garage," Roxy whispered. "If we cut through the garden, we might be able to get a better look."

Jane glanced around nervously. "What if somebody sees us?"

"We'll tell them we're out for a walk," Roxy reasoned.

"In someone else's garden?" Jane asked.

Roxy rolled her eyes. "I'll say I'm a horticulturist and that I'm checking the soil around here because I want to plant a rare English flower, okay?"

"But—"

"Jane, if you don't shut up and get on with this, somebody *will* see us. Now come on!" Roxy started to tiptoe through the garden.

Reluctantly Jane followed. They managed to creep through the garden without incident and came upon a clearing near the garage.

Roxy pointed towards a steep, grassy incline next to the garage. "If we climb up there, we'll be able to look through that window and see inside," Roxy whispered.

Secretly Jane wanted to turn back, but they had come this far already. It would be stupid to pack it in now.

Roxy made her move, Jane right behind her. They stayed close together as they inched up the incline below the window.

Millie was in her family's garage, surrounded by stolen banners reading YO, JANE RYAN! and DEREK FOR PREZ – THE ONLY WAY TO VOTE. Someone was with her – a teenage boy. But Jane didn't recognise him. "Who's that?" she asked.

Roxy clamped a hand over Jane's mouth. "Shh!" She was staring through the window at Millie and her mystery friend, her eyes as wide as saucers.

Jane removed Roxy's hand from her mouth.

"I've seen that guy before," Roxy whispered. "He works at the printing company you sent me to. He's the one I gave the order to. *After* I proofed it."

Jane peered in at Millie and the guy as everything started to take shape in her mind. Millie had sent her to Street Smart Graphics because she had an insider there who could make sure that nothing came out the way Jane wanted it to. Millie was behind everything. What a two-faced snake! How could she pretend to be Jane's friend and do all these horrible things?

Roxy started to shriek and point.

Jane covered her sister's mouth just in time.

Millie and the boy from Street Smart were totally making out!

Roxy went to work with her digital camera, capturing the stolen banners in every shot. After all, a picture was worth a thousand words. And Jane could think of a few choice ones for Millie McDonnell right now.

"Got it," Roxy whispered. She slipped her hands into the front pockets of her hoodie and pulled out the eggs.

"No, forget it," Jane said, and she made Roxy put the eggs away. "Let's just get out of here." The more distance she had between herself and Millie right now, the better. Her friend had totally betrayed her, and it hurt.

Jane and Roxy carefully crept down the incline, slipped through the garden, and raced to the street.

"Millie is going *down*," Roxy said.

Jane started to relax a little bit, knowing that the car was only a block away.

Flashing blue lights lit up the night like fireworks, and Jane and Roxy froze. *Not again*, Jane thought.

A police car cruised up beside them. "Do you girls live around here?"

"Yes," Roxy said. "We're just out taking a walk."

"Well, you know, there's been a lot of vandalism around here lately," the officer said. "What's your address?"

"Oh, we live on the next street over," Roxy improvised – badly.

"What's the name of the street, miss?" the officer pressed.

"Uh… Chestnut Street?" Jane said.

"Okay," the officer said. "Have a nice night."

"Thanks. We will," Roxy said, bending down to tie one of her shoelaces, which had come undone. That's when the eggs fell out of her pockets. "Oops."

"Hold it," the officer commanded. "What were you planning to do with those eggs?"

"Officer, we can explain everything," Jane began.

"You can explain it downtown," he replied.

Jane shut her eyes. Could this night get any worse? First she found out her friend was an evil snake, and now she and Roxy were going to jail!

13

Jane slumped on the holding cell bench with her sister. It was true. Jane Ryan was in jail. But not for something virtuous like a passionate political protest. No, she had to get thrown into jail under suspicion of vandalism! Okay, if that wasn't the most humiliating thing on earth, then she didn't know what was.

"I can't believe you actually got me thrown into jail," Jane said.

"You're blaming *me*?" Roxy shot back. "Let's review. *You* come to me to get proof that *your* friend has turned into Dr. Evil. So how is this my fault?"

"The eggs," Jane reminded her. "Whose idea was it to bring those?"

The cop who'd hauled them in started to laugh. "You girls are hysterical. I should grab a bag of popcorn. This is quite a show."

Jane jumped up and gripped the bars with both hands. "We are not here to entertain you! We are innocent!"

The officer chuckled. "On that side of the cell bars, you don't look so innocent."

"Excuse me, do we look like the kind of girls who go around vandalising people's homes?" Roxy asked.

The officer narrowed his eyes. "Yup."

"Well, if we had any intention of vandalising anything, don't you think we would've had more on us than a pair of night-vision goggles and two eggs?" Jane asked.

The officer's face took on a thoughtful expression. Jane felt a glimmer of hope. Maybe she was getting through to him.

But then Prescott the rookie sauntered into the holding area, killing the moment. "I was sitting at my desk doing all of Martin's paperwork when I heard they were bringing you two in. Still *not* shoplifting?"

Jane wanted to scream. "Ugh. That's all we need right now – another officer who doesn't believe us."

"Yeah," Roxy added sarcastically. "Especially an officer as smooth as Prescott."

Prescott's face turned as red as a beet. "These two have been giving me and Martin quite the run around," he told the officer. "Martin had me put on night-shift desk duty again because of these two." He stepped closer to the cell, and chuckled awkwardly through his embarrassment. "But it looks like I might end up winning this round. Not a real cool move on your part."

Roxy gave a pleading look to the officer. "Before we decide who wins, don't Jane and I get a phone call or something?" Then she turned back to Jane and smiled. "But I did like his idea about the cool move though."

"Ohhhh, no," Jane said, knowing exactly what her sister's smile meant. "Roxy, don't you dare!"

Roxy unstrapped her digital camera from her wrist. "Did someone say *dare*?" she asked, and she snapped a picture.

Click.

"Roxy!" Jane cried.

Another officer stepped into the holding area. "Hey, Rick, a call just came in. Travis and Adam picked up three teens in Stone Water Bend. They had toilet paper, baseball bats, water balloons filled with black ink – the whole nine yards." He tilted his head toward Jane and Roxy. "Doesn't sound like these girls are your vandals."

Jane tried to rattle the bars. "I told you that! Let us out of here!"

"Just sit tight," the officer named Rick told them. "Nobody's going anywhere until we get more information." He slipped out of the holding area.

Now it was just Jane, Roxy and Prescott.

The clumsy rookie stared at the sisters through the bars. "Martin thinks I can't handle patrols yet because of you two, and he cut my first ride-along week short by five days. If you manage to get yourself out of this one, then I will make it my personal mission to bring you to justice."

Roxy rolled her eyes. "Okay, this is *so* not a cheesy revenge movie on pay-per-view cable."

Prescott got that shaky look again, and then left the holding cell area, leaving Jane and Roxy there to wait out the real vandals.

"Wow, that guy better hope for some good training before they put him back on the streets," Jane said.

Roxy nodded. "Yeah, he's definitely a long way from being NYPD Blue material."

The girls waited in the cell for another thirty minutes before the officers finally returned with three rough-looking teens shackled in handcuffs – two guys and a girl.

Jane and Roxy did a double take, looked at each other, and shouted in unison, "The klepto!"

Long Island's most notorious shoplifter scowled back at them.

Jane noticed a bulge in one of Shanna's back pockets, a shape which resembled her my-Satellite. "Officers!" Jane shouted. "That girl stole something from me last week, and I can see it right there in her pocket!"

When one of the officers looked at her pointedly,

Shanna wiggled her fingers into her back pocket. Sure enough, she had the my-Satellite. "I didn't steal anything from that girl. This belongs to me. My father works for the company that makes them."

"If that's the case, then why is my name and contact information printed on a label inside the battery door?" Jane asked, and Shanna began to look worried.

One of the younger arresting officers grabbed the my-Satellite to verify Jane's claim. He opened the battery door, looked at Shanna, then at Jane, then at the other officers. "It says 'Property of Jane Ryan' clear as day."

Jane and Roxy's arresting officer shook his head. "Give her back the gadget, and let those two go. The only thing they're guilty of is annoying me, and my own kids do that every single day. I don't keep them in jail." He laughed at his own joke, then said to Jane, "Unless you want to press charges for the theft, miss. In which case we'll need to take your gizmo for evidence."

Jane shook her head no, thrilled to finally have her my-Satellite back. But the moment Officer Rick placed it in her hands, she knew something was wrong. The screen was completely blank. She made a series of entries and conducted a battery of quick tests. Still nothing. All her data was gone. Jane glared at Shanna. "You broke it!"

Shanna scowled. "Don't look at me. It made a funny noise this afternoon and just stopped working. That thing is a piece of junk."

Jane wanted to scream. Her election schedule... her *life* schedule! Now she would never get them back!

14

NO MATTER WHAT, DON'T BITE YOUR
NAILS.

That was at the very top of Jane's handwritten list
of daily reminders. She took a deep breath. *Wait a
minute. Was deep breathing on there?* she asked herself
and scanned the paper.

TAKE DEEP BREATHS.

Okay. Number three, she thought.

Babette came rushing up to Jane. "Oh, my God!
Have they finished counting the votes yet? Please tell
me they've finished counting. They've *got* to be
finished counting the votes! How long does it take to
count the votes?"

Jane leaned back against her locker and closed
her eyes. "Babette, this is not helping my stress level at
all."

"I just can't believe that the election is so close!"
Babette went on. "It's like *American Idol*! By the way,
my parents won't let me watch that anymore. They

say it makes me too tense."

The election had been held yesterday, but they were still counting the votes. That's how narrow the margin was. The new senior class president of South Side High would be winning by just a few ballots.

And deep down Jane had to admit that she probably wouldn't be in the running were it not for Roxy's little jailhouse trick. The photo of Jane Ryan behind bars had earned her the "Cool Move of the Week," and she had become the talk of the school.

"Yo, Jane Ryan!" the captain of the swimming team shouted from down the hall, holding up the school newspaper with her picture plastered on the front page. "Way to live life on the edge!"

Meanwhile Babette babbled on. "I still can't believe that Millie did all that to you! It's so wrong! It's beyond wrong! There's never been anything more wrong!" Babette hesitated. "Except for this! Do you know what I heard? Even though Millie dropped out of the race, there are still some kids who voted for her as a write-in candidate! What is wrong with people?"

Just as Jane felt a scream rising in her throat, Roxy came to the rescue.

"Babette, do you know what the great thing about having a twin is?" Roxy asked, taking Babette's arm and gently but firmly leading her away. "You totally know when the other half is about to have a complete meltdown."

Jane breathed a sigh of relief. She checked her watch again. Principal Paige would be issuing the final count any minute now…

Thoughts of Millie still bothered Jane. It hurt that someone she'd thought of as a close friend could secretly harbour such bitter feelings towards her. But instead of dwelling on the negative, Jane concentrated on appreciating the good wishes and kindness of sincere friends. That was a little tip she'd learned from reading Congresswoman Kelso's book, *Run to Win*.

The loudspeaker crackled. "Good afternoon, students of South Side High. I have the results of the senior class presidential election. It was a very close race. Our new president will take office by the slimmest margin in our school's history – seven votes."

Jane gasped. Her heart pounded in her chest.

From out of nowhere Derek appeared and slipped his fingers through hers. "Good luck," he said.

She smiled at him, feeling much less anxious now. Whatever happened, she would be happy. For herself, or for him.

Jane stood frozen at her locker. The outcome of the election was just seconds away. So was her chance of winning the McGill Fellowship. She squeezed Derek's hand.

All the students in the hall stopped in their tracks, awaiting the final word.

"And the new senior class president of South Side High is… Jane Ryan!"

Whoops and cheers erupted in the corridor.

Jane could hardly believe it. The whole experience was surreal, as if it were happening to someone else. She'd won! She'd actually won!

Roxy, Babette, and throngs of friends came running up to her, hugging her and screaming congratulations. But the best part of all was Derek. He seemed to be the most excited of all. Proof positive that she had found a class act and supergreat guy. In fact, he wouldn't even let go of her hand.

"You're really on your way, Jane," Derek said. "Congratulations."

"I'm the class president," she replied. "I guess that means I can give some orders now."

Derek grinned. "I guess it does."

"Then I hereby order you to kiss me," Jane said.

Derek pulled her in close. "And I would never think of disobeying my president."

Jane leaned into the kiss… and it was magic.

15

Late that afternoon Jane dropped by Congress-woman Kelso's re-election headquarters to deliver the great news. She found the hardworking candidate in her office, shoes off, stockinged feet propped up on her desk.

"Jane! Forgive my appearance, but I'm exhausted. I just finished an outdoor rally. Great crowd. Energy was electric. But I'm wiped."

"You work too hard," Jane remarked.

"No rest until election day. That's an important rule." Congresswoman Kelso searched Jane's face. "I see a twinkle in your eye," she said. "You won, didn't you?"

Jane smiled and nodded excitedly.

Congresswoman Kelso raised both fists in the air. "Oh, Jane! This is wonderful! Your first election win! I'm so happy for you! This should go a long way towards convincing the review committee that you're McGill Fellowship material." She paused a beat.

"And so should the letter of recommendation I sent off to the chair."

"Oh, thank you, thank you, *thank you*!" Jane exclaimed. "Your support means so much to me, Congresswoman."

"Jane, you've worked very hard, and you've performed invaluable services around here. I consider you a colleague now. And my colleagues call me Kate."

Jane was floored by the acknowledgment. She straightened her spine. "Well… *Kate*, thank you very much!"

The congresswoman laughed.

Beep. Beep. Beep.

The noises were coming from inside the congresswoman's purse. She scowled at the source. "That reminds me. I think there's a technical glitch in the my-Satellites," she said. "Some units have a bad chip in the circuit board that erases all data without warning. It's nonretrievable too. I don't know why I still have mine. I should just throw it into the Hudson River."

"I'm painfully aware of the glitch," Jane said.

"Oh, no!" the congresswoman exclaimed. "Not yours too! It happened to Tim's unit as well, but my husband promises me that the kinks are being worked on. I'll get you another one."

"No thanks," Jane said, holding up her brand-new day planner. It was already bulging with contact numbers, To Do lists, and her *new* life schedule. "I've learned my lesson. From now on I'm organising myself the old-fashioned way – on paper. After all, nothing could go wrong with paper, right?"

mary-kateandashley

(1)	It's a Twin Thing	(0 00 714480 6)
(2)	How to Flunk Your First Date	(0 00 714479 2)
(3)	The Sleepover Secret	(0 00 714478 4)
(4)	One Twin Too Many	(0 00 714477 6)
(5)	To Snoop or Not to Snoop	(0 00 714476 8)
(6)	My Sister the Supermodel	(0 00 714475 X)
(7)	Two's a Crowd	(0 00 714474 1)
(8)	Let's Party	(0 00 714473 3)
(9)	Calling All Boys	(0 00 714472 5)
(10)	Winner Take All	(0 00 714471 7)
(11)	PS Wish You Were Here	(0 00 714470 9)
(12)	The Cool Club	(0 00 714469 5)
(13)	War of the Wardrobes	(0 00 714468 7)
(14)	Bye-Bye Boyfriend	(0 00 714467 9)
(15)	It's Snow Problem	(0 00 714466 0)

HarperCollins*Entertainment*

PARACHUTE PRESS

DUALSTAR PUBLICATIONS

mary-kateandashley.com
AOL Keyword: mary-kateandashley

mary-kate and ashley
TWO of a kind ™

(16) Likes Me, Likes Me Not — (0 00 714465 2)

(17) Shore Thing — (0 00 714464 4)

(18) Two for the Road — (0 00 714463 6)

(19) Surprise, Surprise! — (0 00 714462 8)

(20) Sealed with a Kiss — (0 00 714461 X)

(21) Now you see him, Now you don't — (0 00 714446 6)

(22) April Fool's Rules — (0 00 714460 1)

(23) Island Girls — (0 00 714445 8)

(24) Surf Sand and Secrets — (0 00 714459 8)

(25) Closer Than Ever — (0 00 715881 5)

(26) The Perfect Gift — (0 00 715882 3)

(27) The Facts About Flirting — (0 00 715883 1)

(28) The Dream Date Debate — (0 00 715854 X)

(29) Love-Set-Match — (0 00 715885 8)

(30) Making a Splash — (0 00 715886 6)

HarperCollins*Entertainment*

PARACHUTE PRESS

DUALSTAR PUBLICATIONS

mary-kateandashley.com
AOL Keyword: mary-kateandashley

mary-kateandashley

mary-kateandashley

Sweet 16

(1) *Never Been Kissed*	(0 00 714879 8)
(2) *Wishes and Dreams*	(0 00 714880 1)
(3) *The Perfect Summer*	(0 00 714881 X)

HarperCollins*Entertainment*

PARACHUTE PRESS

DUALSTAR PUBLICATIONS

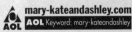
mary-kateandashley.com
AOL Keyword: mary-kateandashley

The New Addition To Your Collection

the mary-kate and ashley brand

Fab freebie!

You can have loads of fun with this ultra-cool Glistening Stix from the **mary-kate**and**ashley** brand.
Great glam looks for eyes, lips – or anywhere else you fancy!

All you have to do is **collect four tokens from four different books from the mary-kate**and**ashley brand** (no photocopies, please!), send them to us with your address on the coupon below – and a groovy Glistening Stix will be on its way to you!

Go on, get collecting and sparkle like a star!

Real Books for Real Girls

It's What **YOU** Read